Index of

Death of a Salesman……….4

Elementary…………………..69

The Problem at Witney...112

Mass Murder………………….149

Copyright 2020 by William Todd

All rights reserved This book or any portion thereof may not be reproduced or used in any manner whatsoever without the express written permission of the author and publisher except for the use of brief quotations in a book review.

Printed in the United States of America.

First printing, 2020.

Print and ebook editions available via Kindle Direct Publishing.

Foreword

Over the course of our friendship, which has lasted for several decades now, I have been privileged to be involved personally in hundreds of cases my friend Sherlock Holmes has put to successful conclusions. So many that the volumes it would take to put them all into print would be a monumental undertaking that I fear I could never accomplish in the amount of time Providence has dictated I have left in this world. There are more than a few cases that, although inspiring awe with his utter brilliance of deduction, they will nonetheless remain only as a memory due to promises kept to the person or government involved which could put peoples' lives in jeopardy even all these years after the fact.

Yet, there are also stories which showcase Holmes's remarkable abilities, perhaps in a simpler form—the charcoal sketches among his Rembrandts. It is these cases that I often look upon most fondly, if only because my mortal mind can more easily understand their uncomplicated splendor. As I go through my files on this cold winter's night, sitting by a roaring fire with some of these stories scattered about me on the floor or in my hand, they bring back a rumination. A fond memory of the case itself, surely, and the intricate methods used by Holmes to bring it to a proper termination, of course, but also—and perhaps more importantly to me—they bring back recollections of a more youthful friendship that warm me in these waning days.

Here are four such cases that are remarkable to me, even now, and I hope my readers enjoy them set forth for the first time. **Dr. John Watson**

Death of a Salesman

I had long planned a holiday to the Cornish coast, but it seemed that either time or circumstance had always prevented it, especially in the warmer months. The late summer had been a warm and dry one and, seeing that I had time on my hands and a willing cover for my practice while away, I endeavoured to finally take that holiday.

I had long been fascinated by the rugged beauty and steep coastal cliffs of the Penwith Peninsula and had been told at a medical conference by a colleague who'd had the pleasure of staying there of Kerrek House, an ancient and dilapidated manor and adjacent tin mine that had been recently restored and turned into a hotel. Although Kerrek House's esteemed history was intriguing, it was by no means its only, and I daresay primary, allure. It sat not one-hundred feet from one of the steepest and sheerest cliffs in all of England, Folly's End. It seemed from that height one could see the entirety of the Great Atlantic.

I had asked my friend, Sherlock Holmes, if he had sufficient pause in his investigations to accompany me for a few days. He initially balked at the idea of exchanging the invigorating stimuli of London for the idleness of the countryside, for he abhorred mental stagnation. Anticipating his usual detestations, I had also coincided my holiday with a BBKA (British Beekeepers Association) symposium in nearby Newquay. At hearing this, he acquiesced.

On the day of departure, I presented myself with my luggage while Holmes was sipping tea, reading the BBKA brochure in a chair next to the window that opened onto Baker Street below. He had a boyish excitement in his eyes. He waved the brochure at me, "Hallo, Watson, my good man. Did you know they are going to have some Epeoloides pilosulus on display at the symposium? The rare cuckoo bee from

America. I was just going through the mail on the side table and found the pamphlet just in time."

"I gave you that brochure two weeks ago," I remonstrated, "and you are just now getting around to reading it?"

"He waved off the statement. "Surely, just knowing about the symposium was enough for me, but having Epeoloides pilosulus on hand to examine is the cherry on the cake."

"Where are your things?" I asked, having noticed that Holmes had no luggage of his own out.

Glancing up at the clock on the mantle, Holmes replied, "My dear Watson, we are not leaving for another hour for the station. I have plenty of time to get my things packed. We will only be gone four days. I only require a few things to satisfy my wants. Unlike—" at this, he waved his hand at my three pieces of luggage.

"Well, I prefer to pack for contingencies. It is a compulsion I learned in Afghanistan and one that has served me well."

Holmes sighed, drank the rest of his tea and stood. "As you wish, Watson. I shall prepare as if we were to be stranded cliff-side for months, even though my primary dress will be my beekeeper's outfit."

. . . . .

In an hour and a half, we were on the Great Western Railway, on our way out of Paddington to Newquay, and from there a taxi to Kerrek House.

Within an hour of departure, it was time for luncheon, so Holmes and I made our way to the dining car for tea and sandwiches. It was a bright and airy car with butter-coloured oak panels and tulip-shaped sconces with mirrored backing placed at intervals to give one the feeling of picnicking in a field of wildflowers. We took a small booth in the middle of the car next to a waist-high railing, arched in the middle, that separated the dining car into equal halves.

Holmes seemed to be in one of his fasting moods, a habit he espoused to keep his mind sharp; however, I partook of a salmon and cream cheese sandwich with my tea. Holmes seemed content to sip his cup and watch with a studious eye the people around us.

"The world holds myriad curiosities if one would but observe them, wouldn't you say, Watson?"

"I would agree," I replied, "but I daresay someone like you sees much more than the average person, ergo, you see more curiosities."

Still casting his gaze about, he idly waved off my statement. "Do we not all have eyes? The problem is everyone sees, not everyone *observes*." With a surreptitious nod of his head, he led me in the direction of a couple a decade our seniors, by the look of them, a few tables down on the opposite side of the aisle. She had a boisterous voice as plump as her cheeks. Her hair was a monsoon of red curls that bounced as she spoke. The gentleman across from her was very animated, as well, when he spoke, whose gesticulations seemed to mimic the woman's hair. He had thinning brown hair and a wiry mustache. "For example," he went on, "I can deduce just from observation that the man is a printer, possibly calico by the alizarin dye on his fingers that has not come completely clean. He has a Wirehair Terrier who bid his master goodbye before he left, and he is also hiding the fact that he is married and has been for quite some time and does not wish his companion to know."

"And you can tell all this how?" I asked.

"The terrier is easy. He has several hairs on his trouser leg. The height up from his shoe tells me it is a small dog. The thickness, texture, and color relays to me the breed—it is a Wirehair Terrier. Simple observation. Now, onto the not-so-simple yet equally correct: He does his best to keep his left hand out of view while they talk. See how he keeps it resting on his knee, yet he is quite dynamic with his other hand. He holds his trouser leg to keep from bringing that hand up and into view as he speaks. And can you see the indentation left by the wedding ring?"

I turned briefly and strained my eyes to look without being too obvious (for the couple was at an odd angle to my seat) and agreed. "Yes, I can see it. Maybe he is a recent widower and has just taken off his wedding ring."

Holmes shook his head in disappointment. "Then where is his mourning band? And his actions clearly are not those of widower. Observe, Watson, don't just see. His finger is still red from the mighty task of removing it just before he came into the dining car. He did not immediately sit down with the lady but asked if he could join her only after sitting by himself momentarily, then, when seeing she was alone, asked to sit with her for company. This I observed while you were ordering your tea and sandwich. I know he has been married for quite some time for the finger's girth grew along with his waistline over the years, which is why it was so hard to remove. His wife takes good care of his needs as evidenced by his starched shirt and ample midsection, yet he is no longer satisfied. The eternal and innate disease of impiety has infected this man's soul, and his wedding vows shall now suffer the consequences. And notice upon whom he has decided shall remedy that illness. She is younger than him but not by much. She is as equally soft and ample around the middle as her suiter. Rather plain, if not a bit homely—"

"Holmes!"

"—So, if this gentleman is being flirtatious with a woman of this caliber, then it can be assumed that his wife is of a similar pedigree, possibly a bit less…comely. And she is probably a vociferous talker, as well."

"Come, now, Holmes. You are delving into the realm of idle speculation, now. There is no way you can deduce that based on the man's girth and ring finger."

He smiled. "Possibly, Watson, yet Bain's psychology suggests that after time, one subconsciously gravitates toward the familiar. So even though this man is unsatisfied with his situation, without realizing his actions he is attracted to someone with similar traits as his wife—frowzy, loud—with but one exception: she is not his wife. And this inclination towards the familiar can only take place after quite some time of indoctrination. That and his relative age also lend themselves to my deduction that he has been married for some time. Bain is incorrect in some of his premises, but not this; with this, there can be no doubt."

I could only shake my head. "Honestly, Holmes. I don't know whether to be flabbergasted at your thought process or pity it. Would it not be easier and less taxing to look over at them and think, 'there is a couple having a nice time together'?"

"I do not make the truth, Watson, I only observe it. Something of which you should try harder to accomplish. Either I am a terrible teacher, or you are a terrible student, and I daresay the former cannot be so." He then turned to me with a wry smile. "Quickly, Watson, salvage my abilities of edification—how many tables are in this car? Do not look, keep your gaze on me. No cheating."

I put down my sandwich. "Well, let me think." I closed my eyes as I tried to visualize the dining car's layout in my mind, counting the tables. "I believe they are set about at regular intervals, keeping the same configuration on both sides, the aisle in the middle. I believe there are…ten tables present and four booths, one on each side of the railing on both sides."

"Bravo, Watson!"

I opened my eyes. "So, I was correct, then?"

Holmes smiled. "You were not. But you were only off by two. I commend you on the attempt, however. You did what you should have done—pictured it in your mind. No doubt you failed to count the two small tables on either side of the door to the kitchen, each holding large bouquets of roses."

I started to object, but Holmes held up a quieting hand. "I said *tables*, Watson, not just dining tables. Observe, do not just see. Something as simple as counting the tables should have been an almost unconscious act. Ah, but the true test comes with remembering the finer details."

"And you did that when we came in, I suppose?"

"Then and in the interim, of course. To me, it is as natural as breathing."

"Then, you won't mind a little assessment," said I as I wiped my mouth on my napkin.

He gave me a look as if daring me to test him. "Are you a betting man, Watson?"

"Ah, a little wager, then? Alright." I felt comfortable enough that there had to be something or someone in the coach that had escaped his gaze.

"The winner buys lunch?"

Knowing that buying Holmes any meal would cost me next to nothing with his bird-like eating habits I agreed. "Alright, then…" I looked around the coach, looking for a suitable target to test Holmes's observational skills. Of course, his deductive skills never ceased to amaze me, but recalling details of an unfamiliar place with unfamiliar people after only twenty minutes seemed a stretch even for the great detective. The car at the front nearest the kitchen was full of patrons chatting, eating, and drinking, but they were in Holmes's direct line of sight. I tried to pick the most nondescript person in the coach and someone who, preferably, was at his back.

"Alright, please describe to me the people sitting at the fifth table on right."

Holmes took a deep breath and closed his eyes, momentarily, putting his hands together under his chin introspectively. Then, he opened his eyes, casting his gaze ahead in recollection. "Do you mean the fifth table on the right as we came in or from the other direction? No matter. They both only have one occupant. Nice try at subterfuge, my good fellow. I shall assume you meant the gentleman at the fifth table down from our entrance."

I sighed for I already knew I had lost the wager.

"He is a slight fellow. Young. Sandy hair. A grey sack suit. Side whiskers, but I believe his face is stubbled, so he left his residence this morning without a shave. His otherwise unblemished countenance probably means that he was running late. Given a choice of grooming habits to forsake, he chose shaving. He is single for his wife would not have let him leave unshaven or tardy. I would deduce that he made arrangements for this train at the last minute. He is pretending to read a book, but he is really studying someone else in the car because on more than one occasion I had noticed him look up from his book. His gaze was intent, holding within it malice of some substance, and it was directed towards someone at the opposite end of the car. I would suggest that he is an office worker of some sort. Definitely not manual labor. He is too slightly built, and his hands are too clean."

He redirected his gaze upon me, smiling in that manner that does not entirely hide an air of superiority. "Well, Watson, how did I do?"

Shaking my head, I replied, "Well, I guess I deserved that." Trying to save even a small amount of dignity, I then added, "But what was he reading?"

With feigned exasperation, Holmes declared, "Really, Watson!" He summoned over the waiter to reap his reward, I hoped just a cucumber and cream cheese sandwich. "He is reading, *Man and His Kingdom*. The script is too small to make out the author, however, I am sure you will grant me that one small failure." To the waiter, he then said, "May I see a menu. I am famished."

As we waited on Holmes' substantial meal, a man approached us from the front of the car. He was a dapper dresser, clean-shaven and wore an impossibly large, if not slightly exaggerated smile. Stopping at our table, he removed his brown trilby, revealing close-cut dark hair. He introduced himself as he ran his fingers along its narrow brim, restlessly. "Good afternoon, gentleman. I do hope you forgive the intrusion, but you look like men of distinction. I am Newbury, Collin Newbury. I am an agent of McAllister and Sons Tailors, on my way to Cornwall on business. I couldn't help but notice, and please forgive my imprudence, that your attire seems a bit…démodé."

His was the smooth, quick-paced tenor of a street vendor, with an irritatingly bumptious air, and I was about to voice my displeasure at my attire being insulted and for being pitched to at a meal table, when Holmes shot me a look from the corner of his eye as he held back the tiniest of grins. It was a look that told me he had this well in hand.

"Please, go on," said my friend with fabricated interest.

"Thank you, sir," he said with a slight bow. "Now, I wear a suit made by McAllister and Sons,"—at this, his ran his fingers along the lapels of the dark-materialed and pin-striped suit—"and you might think this was personally tailored to my exact measurements. But you would be mistaken, my good man. This was bulk manufactured at our modern facility in London. We can now bring well-tailored suits to the masses for a fraction of the cost. If either of you two gentlemen might be interested in trying on one of these fine pieces of attire, I happen to have three more samples of differing sizes of this very suit. Would either of you be interested in updating your wardrobe?" He winked at Holmes. "The ladies will be at your feet. They can't resist a well-dressed man, especially one with continental fashion."

"As much as I appreciate the sentiment," retorted Holmes, "Ladies are the last thing I want at my feet. As far as the suit is concerned—" at this he quickly felt the man's lapel

"— I can tell by a quick study that it is made from a thinner material, possibly cotton broadcloth, suclat, perhaps. Soft but not the durable wool of my frock coat. Yours is only single-stitched while mine is double-stitched, which means yours will not last as long, which also means that were I to switch out my wardrobe for McAllister and Sons, I would have to spend more money constantly buying new suits to replace the worn ones to have, as you say, *'ladies at my feet'*. And you are wearing fillers under your coat to make it more form-fitting and therefore look more personally tailored. Indeed, if that is what one must do to attract the fairer sex these days, I want no part of it. And all that time and money wasted when I could have just stuck to my démodé attire. Thank you but no."

At this, I heard the three young ladies at a table across from us snicker at Holmes's rebuffs of the man's sales pitch.

The man, Mr. Newbury, glanced behind him at the group of women then back at Holmes. "As you wish, sir," he said, displaying rather an unwounded, almost insouciant countenance. "You cannot blame a man for trying. I bid you good afternoon."

The man slowly returned to his table and only stared out the window silently and sipped at his cup.

"Indeed, Holmes! I'm surprised you wasted your time on that dandy-dressed carnival barker," said I. "It serves him right to embarrass himself in front of those ladies, trying to pass off inferior tailoring as fashion."

Holmes chuckled. "Indeed, I doubt I wounded him at all. He seemed rather impervious by my critique. I'm certain I am not the first to point out those flaws. But alas, mass-production is the future, Watson. Soon, we will all be wearing sackcloth as evening wear."

"But to insert one's self into someone else's conversation and meal," I lamented. "Is fashion really so serious to consider?"

"Among those who have nothing more serious to consider," he replied.

My friend took a sip of his tea, then added. "Still, our little encounter was better than reading *Man and His Kingdom,* wouldn't you say? Speaking of our diminutive example of recollection skills, where did he go?"

"The man was at your back. How on earth did you know he left?"

Holmes smiled at me. "Because I know your observational skills are not what they should be, Watson. There is a mirrored sconce right in front of me on the archway. I can see quite clearly everything at my back, and I deduced that you would pick someone out of my line of sight. It was all quite simple from there."

"You cheated!" I remonstrated. "You should pay for your own lunch, especially with the abundance you ordered."

"Ah, Watson, a bet is a bet," he laughed. "Besides, recollection and observation are two sides of the same coin. I did not cheat. I observed that there was within my purview something that could aid me in my recollection. I simply used it as a means to an end. In investigation, one must use *all* the tools at his disposal. And I now observe that during our exchange with the salesman, our young gentleman left the dining car." He then squinted with determination into the mirror. "Alas Watson, I can also see that he must have dropped something from his trouser pocket. I see a piece of paper, newsprint, I think, on his empty chair."

Holmes got up and went to the chair a few tables from us and retrieved the paper. Sitting back down, he remarked as he unfolded it, "Maybe Mr. Newbury should have been making his pitch to this young fellow, instead of us. His trouser pocket was too open and loose, and this fell out as he stood to leave."

It was indeed a cut-out piece of newsprint.

"What do you make of it, Holmes?"

After reading the headline he turned the scrap of newspaper to me. It was an article from the Royal Cornwall Gazette. It read: **Brazen Robbery in St. Austell, £10,000 Stolen from Bank in Early Morning Heist.**

After looking at the headline and noticing the date of the paper, I asked, "What interest would someone have in a robbery that happened almost a year ago to the day?"

"If he carries a newspaper article with him of the event then it must be more than a passing interest. I think you picked the perfect individual for our little experiment, Watson. It was your choice that drew me to him. Now, it seems, he may need a bit more watching."

"But he is gone."

"Yes, however, he is still on the train so I think we can rest easy that we shall not lose him between here and our next stop. Once I eat my ill-gotten gains, we can retire to our cabin for the remainder of the trip to let it digest."

"I still think you should pay for it yourself," I mumbled.

"Tut tut, Watson," Holmes replied with a laugh. "Be a good sport. After all, we are on holiday."

The afternoon passed without event. We returned to our cabin after a rather expensive lunch and there we stayed for the remainder of the trip. I read the paper while Holmes sunk his chin upon his chest as he smoked his clay pipe.

Upon reaching Par, we changed trains to Newquay.

Holmes, ever vigilant, spotted our young man ahead of us as we changed platforms. Pointing discretely, He said, "There's our man, Watson."

We were both surprised when, instead of staying on in Par, which we both were certain would be the case, since St. Austell is just down the coast from there, he boarded the train for Newquay. He was amongst a queue of passengers that included the rebuffed salesman, the young ladies who sat across from us in the dining car, and the older couple having their *affaire de coeur*. In fact, it seemed that many of the passengers from our train were making the transfer to Newquay.

"Maybe the young man will be at your bee symposium," I said as he disappeared up the steps and into the coach.

Holmes *hmph*ed at the statement. "Better he than our fashion garçon."

I shrugged. "It may be possible, Holmes, that we are seeing something that simply is not there."

"It *may* be possible, but it is highly unlikely. There was someone in the dining car who elicited that hateful glare he wore. I could see it on his face. Unfortunately, there were too many people grouped together at the other end of the car for me to tell for whom those icy stares were meant."

"Well, without more facts to put forth, you might as well let it go. It's not as if an angry stare is punishable under the law, and malicious thoughts do not always end up in malicious actions. You have a bee symposium waiting for you, and I have rest and relaxation waiting for me."

As we boarded the train to Newquay, Holmes replied, "Perhaps you are right, Watson…Perhaps."

. . . . .

We, at last, stepped off the platform at our destination. The late afternoon sun was bright and warm. Legion passengers headed for the platform to Penzance or filtered into the station, staying on in Newquay. It was in this helter-skelter of bodies that we lost our quarry. It seemed a nice diversion on the long ride from London to Newquay, but it seemed that the beautiful day and newness of our destination quickly turned our attention back to the solace we had initially sought there.

We retrieved our luggage and made the twenty-minute taxi ride to Kerrek House Hotel.

As we made our way down the one-mile drive to the hotel from the main thoroughfare, a constant wind buffeted our taxi. We were flanked on either side by Cornish oak, all misshapen and leaning obtusely in the same direction, as years of gales off the Atlantic pummeled them into their familiar shapes. They, along with pines and sycamores that dotted the grassy and bosselated expanse, whipped about, and their late-day shadows danced in epileptic fits along the ground.

The manor house, now a hotel, was a bulky monstrosity of granite and glass that dominated the landscape as we approached with the front of the hotel facing away from the prevailing winds. A red awning overhung the main entrance with stewards awaiting the arrival of the guests. A long row of pines, three-deep on the right side of the structure, buffeted a sunken and quite breathtaking garden with footpaths, hedges, and flowers and fauna of all kinds that stretched out for some distance.

The stewards retrieved our luggage, and we followed them into Kerrek House. Before us at the other end of the spacious entrance hall lay a wide ornate staircase with tiles the color of Jade. To our immediate right (which is where our stewards led us) was the hotel receptionist, a young, smartly dressed woman with a long mane of ginger hair and cheerful, blue eyes. "Good afternoon, gentlemen," she said as she readied her register. "To whom do I have the pleasure?"

"Dr. John Watson and Mr. Sherlock Holmes," I replied.

"Ah, yes. Dr. Watson, you will be staying in Room 315 overlooking the ocean in the east wing, and Mr. Holmes, you will be in Room 316 across the hall facing the garden. Here are your keys. I hope you enjoy your stay."

As we were about to leave, she stopped us. "Oh yes, before I forget, if you are interested, there is a tour of Kerrek

House that starts in an hour. A guide will give you access to the residential parts of the manor and a history of the place and area."

"That sounds wonderful," said I.

"It sounds boring," quipped Holmes.

The receptionist smiled sheepishly at us. "It is not compulsory, but many guests do find it enjoyable. Kerrek House has an interesting history. But if you wish, you may stroll the grounds, read in our lovely library, socialize in our pub and restaurant area…or just stay in your room and enjoy the views."

"The latter shall suffice," whispered Holmes to me as we followed our luggage up the gleaming stairs.

Halfway up, I heard a familiar sound behind me. Holmes heard it as well, for we both turned in unison. It was the salesman, Mr. Newbury. He was explicating (or rather hyperbolizing) on the quality of his wares to a steward who was pushing his suit rack to the front desk for check-in. He saw us looking back at him, and he smiled and waved at us. "Hallo, gentlemen!" he called out to us. "See, Providence has brought us together. I shall have you in one of my suits yet!" He did not wait for a response which was not forthcoming and proceeded to give the waiting receptionist his name, as we made the top landing and disappeared down the east wing hallway.

"I can only hope that his quarters are nowhere near ours," said I as we made our respective rooms. "I did not come on holiday only to be browbeaten into buying a suit I have no interest in ever wearing."

Holmes smiled as the steward unlocked his door. "Perhaps if you buy a suit from him, he will leave you alone. Think of it as a trinket brought back from holiday. Only this one cannot be placed on a mantle and admired. It will have to be burned for warmth on a cold winter's night."

I gave a hardy laugh at the remark. "Perhaps when he sees you in your beekeeper's outfit, he'll make it his personal mission to reform your fashion."

With a fallen face, Holmes replied, "Then I shall endeavor to keep myself as far from the man as I can get. Come get me when your tour is over, and we shall have some dinner."

With that, we entered our rooms and closed the doors.

. . . .

Several guests were milling around in the entrance area near the reception desk when I finally made my way down for the tour of the manor-turned-hotel. The group consisted of the animated adulterer from the train and his mistress, the threesome of young women, also from the train, our suit salesman, a young couple who, if their mutual doting was any indication, were recently married, and a few individual men and women: fourteen of us in all. A finely dressed gentleman with thin, grey hair but a full-feathered goatee, stood before the group checking his pocket watch. Mr. Newbury was near the front of the group, probably gauging the right moment to land his sales pitch to the tour guide, so I stayed near the back doing my best to conceal myself from a sales assault by keeping myself behind the bulk of the stout couple.

As I waited for the tour to start, I felt a tap on my shoulder which startled me. "Holmes! What are you doing here? I did not think the tour interested you."

"It does not," he replied. "But one can only stare out a window at seventy-seven different varieties of flowers, fourteen varieties of bushes, a dozen varieties of trees, and seven varieties of arborvitae, for so long. I need stimuli, Watson, and I received all I was to get from the garden."

"It is time for the tour to start," the guide stated in a dry monotone. "Please follow me and be sure to keep up." He motioned for everyone to follow, and like obedient spaniels, we did so.

At first, he showed us our immediate surroundings—the entranceway, the restaurant, the library with its mahogany and high ceiling and innumerable volumes, no doubt left over from when the place was a residence. But the interesting backstory of the house began when we went beyond the glimmering staircase and into the great hall beyond. One side was a queue of tall windows looking out onto the gardens, while on the other wall was displayed an arsenal such as I had never seen before. It seemed every inch was taken with longbows and arrows, maces and axes, knives and swords of every stripe, muskets and bayonets, rifles and pistols, and four sets of armour stood sentried at the four corners of the expanse.

The tour guide began. "Kerrek House was erected in 1630 by Sir Reginald Kerrek. He made his substantial wealth in tin, copper, and arsenic. His most productive mine was Wheal Kerrek, which can be seen through the windows in the restaurant off in the distance. This was his most profitable mine, and he erected Kerrek House to be near it.

"He had two passions—his mines and, as this wall can attest, collecting militaria, and he went to great lengths and great expense in collecting this vast arsenal. By nature, Sir Reginald was uncouth and unceremonious to the point of rudeness and possessed an iron resolve in all matters. His demeanor on more than one occasion had caused much strife for him and his family. But as unrefined as he might have been, he was also staunchly loyal to the crown and was known throughout Cornwall as a defender of the king and a true Royalist. As it was, during the Great Rebellion, he threw his considerable wealth and influence behind Charles I. Unfortunately, at the Battle of Langport, the Round Heads under the leadership of Oliver Cromwell—"

"I believe you mean Fairfax," Holmes interrupted.

Every eye turned to Holmes. Mr. Newbury smiled and waved at us from the front.

I groaned.

"Excuse me?" the tour guide responded.

"It was Fairfax, Sir Thomas Fairfax who led the army at Langport, not Cromwell. Cromwell, I believe, was Lieutenant General of Horse."

"Holmes!" I whispered harshly. "Let the man do his job. Does it matter?"

"It matters to me, Watson. I should think that truth should matter to you and everyone."

The gentleman gave an audible sigh. I could only surmise the amount of times a day, even a week, he gave this tour with this well-rehearsed verse without incident, and here was Holmes questioning the veracity of his knowledge of history.

"That may be so," the guide replied, "but it was Cromwell on horseback with the cavalry that won the day."

"However true that may be, it was not Cromwell who led the army, it was Fairfax. Semantics, my good fellow, can mean the difference between fact and fiction. Words matter. You said, *'Under the leadership of Cromwell'*, when, in fact, Cromwell was not the leader. It was Fairfax. I believe you should amend your script."

The man pursed his lips and stroked his goatee as he struggled to hold back an obvious annoyance. However, to my surprise, he regained his composure like a true gentleman and began again. "Unfortunately, at the Battle of Langport, Cromwell and his cavalry, *under the leadership of Fairfax,* defeated the Cavaliers. Kerrek, who would in no way acknowledge the leadership of the Parliamentarians, was dragged from his house and hanged by clubmen for his stubbornness, though there are whispers that they were forced into the deed by Cromwell himself at the risk of losing property and the defiling of daughters and wives. And it was in this way that no blame could be leveled against the good name of Cromwell."

We then followed the man through a door with a placard that read *no admittance* into a residential area of the manor laid out like a museum tableau. He explained how the widow Kerrek and her adolescent son, William, were allowed to remain in the home, and when she died only a few years later, William became master of Kerrek House and the mines."

All through his dialogue, whenever a silence would fall over the crowd as we made our way from one section to another, we could see Mr. Newbury confer with our guide in hushed tones as he showcased his suit and exaggerated its extravagance at a reasonable price to the now irritated man, who, at one point, slapped Mr. Newbury's hand away when the salesman tried to persuade him to touch the material.

I heard the rotund man in front of us whisper to his lady friend, "That man is such an annoyance. There is not a suit made that can fit me without being properly tailored. Yet, he yipped at my heels endlessly until I just had to be rude and told him to leave me alone."

Without conviction, the woman replied, "Yes, I remember. I was there, too."

"He will end up provoking the wrong bloke with his incessant claptrap and end up with a fat lip if you ask me." Then he added with emphasis, "Or worse."

The three young ladies who had already mocked him once did so again at the guide's objections to his bothersome overtures. At this, Mr. Newbury turned and said something to them which neither I nor Holmes could hear, although, by the slap in the face that followed, we could only surmise it an unsavory reply. The ladies fell back to the back of the crowd, and from that point on Mr. Newbury was a model, if not subdued, patron for the rest of the tour.

Showing us up a staircase an equal in splendor to the one at the entrance, we found ourselves in a large room filled with myriad bolts of fine fabric and a small army of tailor's dummies and several full-bodied mannequins. Upon one wall was a large tapestry of Kerrek House and its surrounding environs. Wheal Kerrek and all its associated tunnels were displayed like a many-legged spider and its web.

Here, we stopped once again.

"William Kerrek," the tour guide expounded, "whose constitution was closer to that of his mother than his father, was a soft soul who loved fine dress as much as fine food."

At this statement, Mr. Newbury cleared his throat rather loudly.

Ignoring him, the guide continued, "Cupid's arrow shows no partiality, and by it he was struck whilst in a most unexpected place; he fell quite head-over-heels in love with the tailor's daughter, Josephine Palk. She, though a right beauty and an equal to her father in tailoring, was well below William's station, and he was warned by family and friends that the arrangement just could not be. But it mattered not to love-struck William Kerrek. Against all advice and pleading, they married, and she, because of her love and proficiency as a clothier, continued to make clothes for the entire family, which numbered eight at its height. For those who might know local history, in this very room, she made the wedding gown for Lady Helena of Bristol. This," he said with a sweep of his hand, "became Josephine's Room. With William running the mines and Josephine clothing the elite of Cornwall, Kerrek House prospered through the beginning of this century before illness, war, and squandering by later generations depleted both the family tree and its wealth. Sadly, the mines closed, and the house boarded up as no Kerreks of this lineage survive today.

"Kerrek House was then bought in 1887 and completely restored, updated, and turned into a hotel by Ciaran Todde, a businessman from Glasgow. He and his family come down each summer and stay for a month in the residential area. They just returned to Scotland only two weeks ago."

The tour ended in a large observatory up a small flight of stairs from Josephine's Room. The four corners of the glass enclosure commanded the most spectacular view I think I had ever seen. One could see, it seemed, all the way to Eternity, from such a height over the ocean. The skeleton of Wheal Kerrek was to the east along the cliff about a half-mile in the distance. To the west, where the cliffs sloped to the sea, pristine beaches and parts of Newquay could be seen well off into the distance. To our backs, the road leading to the hotel serpentined through the many copses of trees and tall grass that dotted the windswept landscape.

The room itself was barren with but a monstrous telescope facing the ocean-side of the room its only occupant. It was said, William would while away the hours looking out over the waves or into the night sky while his wife made her masterpieces of fabric, lace, and buttons in the room below.

Thus, ended our tour.

As we followed the tour guide back to the populated portion of the hotel, Mr. Newbury, tail between his legs, seemed to finally succumb to the constant rejection and ridiculing and lagged behind even myself and Holmes without so much as a look in our direction. The man was in a most pitiable state, yet, however sullen his countenance, I could not bring my empathy to the point of acquiring one of the man's suits to lift his spirits.

Once back in the lobby, as we turned to head back up the stairs to our rooms to change for dinner, Holmes tapped my shoulder and nodded towards the receptionist, a wry grin beginning to crease his aquiline features. "We cannot seem to rid ourselves of our mysterious paper-clipper. See, our man is procuring himself a room."

I glanced in that direction. The young man from the train was filling out the registry in earnest with hurried strokes. "Isn't it odd," I offered, "that he has no luggage."

"It is, indeed, Watson," was Holmes's reply as we made our way up the stairs. "It may be that a black game is being played out before our eyes, and we know not the players nor the object of the game. I fear we may not know the victor until it is too late."

"Shall we just confront the fellow, show him the article, and ask his motives?"

"No, we shall watch from a distance. If he knows he is being watched, it may scare the rabbit back into its hole. If he has dark motives, he may hide them only to bring them forth on another occasion—an occasion with which we shall not be able to help."

As we made the top of the stairs, the young man bounded, two steps at a time, up the stairs past us and down our hallway. He hurriedly unlocked his door as we made the hallway and disappeared into a room at the end of the hallway.

"Knowing where his room is will at least make him easier to keep track of," said my friend.

. . . . .

I awoke the next morning to a grey pall outside my window. Judging its brightness, I knew it must have been first light, and when I consulted my watch it was indeed almost 6:00 a.m. I went to the window as I tried to stretch a kink in my back from an overstuffed mattress to glimpse the vista before me. To my chagrin, the ocean this morning was blanketed by a heavy fog that was lapping at the edge of Folly's End but quickly retreating in the early morning sun

And it was there that I noticed, standing dangerously close to the precipice, Mr. Newbury, still in his pin-striped suit and trilby. He seemed to be mesmerized by the swirling tongues of fog being swept back out to sea. It seemed that the bank was of such a thickness that if one could but leap the distance, they could easily walk across its billowy surface. Maybe he was taking stock of his career choice. Surely there was a more honest situation out there that did not involve trying to peddle inferior product.

What took place next both startled me and made my blood turn cold for out of the glorious morning came death. From out of my line of sight a blur raced across my eyes. That blur landed squarely in Mr. Newbury's back: it was an arrow. The unexpected pain and force from the penetration pushed the man forward awkwardly, and he tumbled over the side of Folly's End.

"Holmes," I whispered. Then, I said it again louder as I turned, threw on my housecoat, and raced to my door, "Holmes, Holmes!"

I ran across the hall and began to pound on the door. It was then that I heard screaming from the floor below.

Holmes was hurriedly putting on his housecoat as he opened the door. "What has happened, Watson?"

"Come," said I. "Newbury just went over the cliff!"

"Suicide?"

"No," I replied. "An arrow through the back was his fate."

As we raced down the hallway, patrons were beginning to poke bleary eyes through open doors, asking from whence the screaming was coming.

We found the source once we made our way to the seating area of the restaurant downstairs. A young woman, by her dress an employee of the hotel, was standing in front of a wall of floor-ceiling windows that looked out at Folly's End a short distance away.

She looked upon us with tears streaming down her face. "I was opening up the curtains, sirs, getting ready for the day and preparing for breakfast, and…and that man, the suit salesman, was just standing there, sirs. I didn't give him much attention, for guests are up at all hours gawking out over the cliffs, like they always do, but usually only at the fenced-off areas. Then, suddenly, sirs, from the corner of my eye I sees him…he…he fell over the side!"

She began to wail, once more.

"Come, Watson!"

We ran out the front entrance and made our way to where Mr. Newbury had been standing, being extremely careful ourselves not to slip in the wet grass and share his fate. We both craned our necks out over the side. The man's lifeless body was floating in the roiling waters several hundred feet below, having finally caught itself up between two large boulders.

Holmes said, "The cliffs on either side extend for at least a mile in each direction, and the waters are too rough at the moment to safely retrieve the body. The constabulary may well have to wait for low tide before Mr. Newbury can be recovered."

He turned and peered up at the hotel. "Which is your room, Watson?"

"Near as I can tell, it is the fifth set of windows from the right."

Holmes's keen eye surveyed the area around. "Then, the arrow would have emerged from the left of your line of sight."

"Yes," said I.

"Then the fatal arrow would have been shot from the front of the hotel."

People were beginning to gather under the awning, and a gentleman in hotel livery started out towards us, but Holmes stopped him. "Please stop where you are and return to the hotel, all of you!"

"I am the manager," he said.

"And I am Sherlock Holmes. This is a crime scene, and I do not want it trampled upon until I've had time to examine it."

At this point in his career, Sherlock Holmes was a name revered across the whole of the empire; at hearing it, the man instantly acquiesced. "Shall I call for the constabulary, then, Mr. Holmes?"

"Not yet. I shall need fifteen minutes outside. Once I've gathered what I can out here then you may send word."

The manager shooed everyone back inside, which left only myself and Holmes. He looked around us, pointing. "The grass is still wet, Watson. It becomes darker where we step. Can you see our footprints left as we ran to the cliff?"

"I can. And there. Those must be Newbury's." Another set could just be made out coming from the gravel drive, across from which was the sunken garden."

"Correct, Watson. And do you not see another set placed very close to his?"

"I do!" I exclaimed as Holmes began to examine the areas.

"I cannot be certain as the indentations are not as prominent as those left in soft soil or mud, but it appears to me that there is a set leading to the cliff, Newbury's, presumably, and one leading away."

"He must have had some clandestine rendezvous," said I.

"I see you've already got your next tale marinating," he offered back waggishly.

"No, no, I'm being quite serious, Holmes. It would fit the facts as we see them right now. It would seem he came out, spoke to someone who must have already been here for some time since I see no second set of prints leading up to the cliff. Newbury was either late to the tete-a-tete or the person needed some time alone to think, but whatever the reason, the second person had to be out here for some time for their tracks leading up to the cliff to be covered by more dew. When he finally arrived, they spoke—quarreled, perhaps. Newbury had a disposition that could certainly rub one the wrong way. The interlocutor left Newbury standing here, those being their footsteps leading away. In a rage for reasons yet unknown, they retrieved a bow and arrow, most likely from the wall of implements inside, and shot Mr. Newbury."

"Well, Watson, since you have this matter in the bag, I shall retire to my room and dress for my bee symposium."

"Come, now, Holmes, stop being so flippant," I remonstrated. "I am just offering a possibility. What do you think?"

"I think I need more data. It may be that you are completely correct in your assumptions, but I do not deal in assumptions. I deal in facts, and I need more clay to make my bricks."

I then followed Holmes, tracing with celerity the dew-darkened footprints to the gravel drive. The options confronting us were going across to the sunken garden or following the gravel drive from the hotel. Deciding on the nearer option, we alighted the four cobblestone steps into the meandering path that wound its way through the garden, and Holmes began pushing aside shrubbery frenetically.

"Hallo, what is this?" he said. He reached between two conical arborvitae and pulled out a longbow. "At least part of your hypothesis is true, Watson. I remember this specimen quite well from the tour and it was shoulder-height upon the wall. Easily obtainable."

I then followed him around, as a hunter does when his hound is on the scent, while he feverishly inspected the gardens for any sign of the murderer's footprints leading out into the surrounding area, however, none were found.

As we made our way back, Holmes remarked, "much of the area in the front, as well as the driveway, is gravel. It would be very easy to escape by that route and not leave a trail. Yet, my belief is the blackguard is among the hotel guests."

"Our news-clipper! You, yourself, said that he was acting very strangely. But what does a clothier have to do with a bank robbery?"

"I think that is a question we need to pose to our strange friend. At this point, I am only certain of one thing, Watson."

"And that is?"

"I shall not be seeing Epeoloides pilosulus today."

When we made our way back into the hotel, the manager, a slight fellow with wideset eyes and a dark, pencil-thin mustache, approached us. He gave Holmes a strange look as we approached, Holmes waving the longbow in his hand.

"Where on earth did you get that?" he asked.

"It was found among the bushes in the garden," Holmes replied.

"Well, why would it be there? It should be among the rest of the implements in the great hall."

Holmes matter-of-factly slapped the longbow on the counter of the reception desk. "This is what killed Mr. Newbury. He was shot in the back with an arrow."

"This wasn't an accident, then?"

"I'm afraid not," replied my friend. "Could you please tell me which room Mr. Newbury was staying in?"

Stricken with the implication of murder, the man's face drained and only stared blankly at Holmes.

"Mr. Newbury's room number, please. And a key to gain entry."

Blinking himself back to reality, the man said, "Yes, yes, right."

He went behind the counter, opened the book, and found the entry. "Mr. Newbury was in 303 in the west wing." He pulled a second key from the corresponding peg on the wall behind him and handed it to Holmes.

"Give me a five-minute head start then call the constabulary and inform them," he instructed the manager. "That should give me enough time to examine the room before the professional forces arrive and ruin any usable evidence. Also, get everyone, patron and employee, into the restaurant and have them sit until authorities arrive. They will want to question everyone on the premises. And have your registry handy. They will want to make sure everyone in the hotel is accounted for."

The manager nodded his ascent.

Before we turned and ascended the stairs Holmes asked, rather off-handedly, "By the way, what time do you begin to serve breakfast?"

"We start serving breakfast at 8:30."

"Thank you."

"Hungry already?" I asked,

"I am rarely hungry at this hour," was his only reply.

We made the top of the stairs and turned left down the west wing of the house. 303 was the third door down on the left. Holmes put out a hand to stop me as we approached the door; it was ajar.

"Someone has beaten us to the punch, Watson," he whispered.

"Shall we wait and watch until the authorities arrive."

"A lion does not wait for the elephant to arrive before pouncing the wildebeest."

"What if he is armed?"

"I shall gauge the situation with stealth. If he is armed, we shall reweigh our options."

We crept to the partially open door. All was silent but for footsteps and the opening and closing of drawers.

"It sounds like he is alone, Watson," my friend whispered to me.

He slowly, quietly, opened the door another few inches until more of the room came into view. It was the young man from the train. He was in a shirt and trousers, and his hands were free, so there was no place on his person to conceal a weapon.

Once ascertaining this, Holmes opened the door boldly. "Why did you kill Mr. Newbury?"

The man said nothing, but his eyes widened, and they held within them a wild and fearful fury, like a cornered animal. He looked madly around, seemingly looking for a way out of the net that was cast around him.

Holmes said, "There is no use. There is one of you and two of us with but one way to escape. I do not think you wish to try and muscle past two men who both outweigh you considerably."

He looked to one than the other of us, thought momentarily, then collapsed onto the bed with his face in his hands.

"I ask again, why did you kill Mr. Newbury?"

He looked at us, confusion transforming his features as if hearing the question for the first time. "Wait, what? Mr. Newbury is dead?"

I replied, "Shot with an arrow in the back, and he went over Folly's End to his death."

"No, no, no, no!" the young man pleaded. He went to the window and looked out. "No!!!" He turned to us. "I only thought he was out to take an early morning stroll in the gardens."

"Why would what Mr. Newbury does matter to you at all?" Holmes asked. "And what does all of this have to do with the St. Austell bank robbery?"

He gave us a knowing look. "Ah, I see you must have come across my keepsake. It troubled me that I had misplaced it."

"I found it in the dining car on the train from London to Par," replied Holmes.

"May I have it back?"

"You may not. Answer the question."

The man sighed. "I shall not. I wish to have a solicitor present."

"Young man, we are not the constabulary, but it would be in your best interest to tell us all you know."

He wrinkled his brow. "If you are not the police then who the deuces are you?"

"I am Sherlock Holmes, and this is my companion, Dr. Watson."

The man's face brightened to the radiance of the sun. "Glory be! Could I really have the blind luck of being in the presence of the great detective?"

With an annoyed sigh, Holmes said, "As I stated…Now, why are you rummaging through a dead man's room, not fifteen minutes after his death, and what does this have to do with a bank robbery on the other side of Cornwall?"

"I do not wish to be at cross purposes, Mr. Holmes, and indeed, I hope that when I am done with my explanation that I may gain your services to my benefit."

"You must make your summation quickly, for the constabulary is on their way. You have less than fifteen minutes."

He began in earnest. "My name is Rory Keene. My sister was Esme Keene. The short version of the story is that she worked at the bank in St. Austell as a teller. She was a pretty girl but not very worldly. She suffered from seizures. She had them often when she was young, but they became more sporadic as she got older. It was hoped that she would eventually outgrow them altogether. Because of her isolated state growing up, she was rather naïve and given over to flights of fancy, which only helped the bank manager manipulate her into doing his bidding. He concocted an idea of them stealing money and eloping together. The facts are fuzzy at this point. Through a means I am not privy to they pulled off the heist and fled across the countryside. At some point, with the police on their heels, Esme injured her ankle as she jumped off a boulder and tumbled down a steep slope. Instead of staying with her, Esme's accomplice left her there, and she was subsequently caught. As she was being brought in for questioning, the whole affair was just too much for her constitution. She had a seizure in the constabulary, one of such extent that she did not recover, and there she died before they could question her. When she was caught, the police gave up their chase on the man for they seemed certain they could get the information they needed to catch him from Esme. When she died, they were left swinging in the wind."

"And who was this bank manager who absconded with the money?" asked Holmes.

"Collin Newbury."

I gasped. "Our dead suit salesman?"

"What makes you think Newbury had anything to do with the robbery?" Asked Holmes.

From his trouser pocket, he retrieved several folded letters and handed them to Holmes. "You see, Mr. Holmes, my sister and I are very close. Our mother died in childbirth, and I am four years older than Esme, so I helped my father with my sister, especially when she was younger, and the fits were upon her often. As I said, as she got older the seizures happened less often, and it was then, with our father, himself now frail and old, that we both took on employment. She went to the bank, and I, feeling the time was now appropriate to do so, went to Canada to apprentice with an uncle who owns three apothecaries. We had been apart for two years, but we wrote each other often. In those letters, she detailed to me their budding romance, her lover's disclosure of his debts (taking care of a drug-addled brother which I now believe a lie). Over time, their plans became more intimate. They wanted to marry, but he was unable to take care of her until he got himself on sounder ground. Apparently, his debts were significant. They saw no other way to repay his debts than to rob the bank. With the proceeds, they would repay the debts and elope to the continent to start their new life together. I tried to persuade her in the firmest language possible how wrong that was, but she was entirely under his spell."

"It sounds as though these letters are material evidence in the robbery," I said. "Why did you not hand these over to the authorities. It could have helped their investigation."

"I did just that, Dr. Watson. But because she never referred to him by name—it was only *my love* and *my gentleman from the bank*—they said it wasn't entirely certain she was referring to Newbury. It could have been a customer for all they knew."

"But you were certain she was referring to Newbury?" Holmes pressed.

"Oh, yes. From previous letters I know there are only three men at the bank, and two are old enough to be her grandfather, one being the owner himself. The rest were women. The process of elimination says it had to be Newbury she was in love with and with whom she was planning this heist and elopement."

"Could it not have been a customer?" I asked.

Keene nodded in agreement. "Yes, but she began working at the bank before I went off to Canada. We were close, you see, and I could tell even from the beginning that she was smitten with Newbury. I am—was—very protective of her. He thought himself a bit of a gal sneaker, and I warned her to be careful around him."

"But he is a suit salesman, now," said I. "What happened?"

"This is how I see it," Keene said. "The papers at the time mentioned that Esme died in custody before implicating her accomplice. Newbury, who had been absent from work for two days suddenly reappeared saying he had taken ill. The police initially investigated him but could prove nothing. He lived alone, and couldn't prove his alibi, but they also could not disprove it. They searched his home, found nothing to implicate him and dropped him as a suspect. He waited for a few months until he was certain he was no longer in their crosshairs, quit the bank, and moved to London where he got the job he now has."

"And you know this how?" asked Holmes.

"The day she was put into the ground I vowed before her and God that I would not stop until I could prove that Newbury was the mysterious accomplice—that the despicable man, even though he did not lay a hand on her, killed my sister. I got my affairs together in Canada, quit my apprenticeship, returned to England, and have been following from afar his every move for the last four months to that end."

"Well, revenge is certainly a motive for seeing him dead," I offered.

He shook his head vociferously. "No, you don't understand. I was not following him to exact revenge. I was hoping he would lead me to the money. I wanted to help resuscitate the good name of Keene. My sister was easily influenced. I do not wish to condone her actions, but I believe it was entirely the idea of Newbury, and under his spell of infatuation, she followed his every whim. If I can find the money and return it, it might put right the wrong she did, and Mr. Newbury will get his just desserts. So, you see, I needed Collin Newbury alive to find the money."

"Then, it would seem," Holmes offered soberly, "that someone else knew about the money and ascertained its whereabouts before you."

"Did you find anything of worth in here?" I asked.

He shook his head despondently, "No. I checked his luggage for any correspondence, maps, anything that might be a clue. I checked the pockets of two of his ghastly suits he has in the wardrobe, and they were empty. I checked the writing desk for any scribbles, along with the wastebaskets, under his sheets and bedding. I've checked everywhere in here, and there is nothing that might lead me to where he's keeping that money."

As Mr. Keene was talking, Holmes went to the window that looked down on the gravel drive at the front of the hotel. "We shall have to resume our conversation at a later time. The constabulary is here. I do not wish to divulge your information to them just yet. It may serve justice better if we work on this little problem without police interference, at least at first. There are times where they are as helpful as an untied shoestring."

He turned back to Mr. Keene. "If you wish to employ my services, you must do exactly as I say."

"I am your puppet, Mr. Holmes. I will follow your instructions to the letter."

"Good. I want you to go down and place yourself amongst the other patrons in the restaurant. When you are interviewed, do not tell them anything of what you have just divulged to us. You are in town for the bee symposium, if they ask your business here. I suspect more than a few will give that same response. I am quite certain they will not wish anyone to leave the premises, and you should acquiesce to that. Go back to your room, and we shall convene there later to get more information, should we need it. Leave the rest of this affair in my hands, and I shall endeavour to bring it to a proper finish."

"I shall do as you say."

Mr. Keene left the room, and we closed and locked the door behind us.

We gave him a head start to the restaurant before we followed. "What do you make of his story?" I whispered as we went down to join the others.

"Intriguing," was the only response Holmes offered.

Instead of seating ourselves in the restaurant with the other hotel guests to wait our fate with the local constabulary, I followed Holmes, who replaced the extra key back onto its peg. Through the windows of the entrance, I could see the manager talking to the police and pointing off to the right, no doubt relaying the horrific events.

Holmes said, "Come, Watson, we might have just enough time for one more quick look before they bring their investigation inside."

We made our way to the great hall of weaponry. He pointed to an empty spot on the wall as we passed. "That, Watson, is from where the weapon was extracted. I only remember it because I am a fan of medieval longbows and was admiring it before I had the misfortune of having my hearing insulted with a dissertation of incorrect history."

Once at the other end, he tried the door to the residential museum of the place. It was unlocked.

"I was hoping for such luck. Come, let us go up to the observation room and surveil the area from that vantage point before we succumb to the annoyance of a police interrogation."

As we walked through Josephine's Room, my friend looked about him with turned brow, I assumed hoping then realizing that we would not be found out by any wandering hotel staff or inquisitive constabulary. He also stopped momentarily and took in the large tapestry upon the wall before he leapt up the stairs two at a time to the observation room.

"Should we swing around the telescope and use it?" I asked.

"No, Watson. Taking the area in broad strokes may be better, at first. If there is anything of note, we may then focus more directly."

He looked around the area, land on three sides and a vast ocean on one. The fog was still of sufficient thickness to be unable to ascertain any boats in the water, but with seas as rough as they were when we looked over the side of Folly's End, none but the largest and sturdiest of vessels would be out this morning.

Holmes then focused on the rocky, windswept area around the hotel and the long-abandoned Wheal Kerrek in the distance. The entire area leading to the cliff was relatively barren, with copses of wood and brush scattered here and there, and high grass whipped in a frenzy in the morning breezes.

His eagle-like gaze scoured over the landscape. "It would be much better to find a trail through the grasses if they would but stay still." After another moment, he snapped, "Confound this wind!" He sighed in resignation and said, "I believe we have seen all we shall see up here."

I followed him back down the stairs. "We are at an impasse, then?"

"Not at all, my good man. Every avenue has its purpose, even if that purpose is to know it leads nowhere."

"Coming up here did no good, then."

"Incorrect, Watson. It revealed more than you realize. My problem at the moment is that I do not know quite yet how to fit together the one or two trifling pieces of this puzzle."

"Do you think our murderer has escaped?"

"It is possible they left by the gravel road, but instinct tells me they are still in the area, possibly sitting in the restaurant below us as we speak."

We finally took our seats away from Mr. Keene, as the constabulary rounded up any stragglers and the Chief Constable, introduced as Penhale, began in earnest with questioning the guests. We waited our turn to be interviewed, while uniformed men searched the area around the hotel. Holmes sighed heavily as he watched through the windows the masses of constables walking over the very evidence they needed to begin to piece together this murder. On occasion, I could see that great brain of his working its machinations as he was either deep in thought or looking around us at the hotel, at the other guests, no doubt piecing together a thought that had just begun to form in my mind: Newbury came to Kerrek House for a reason. The money had to be here somewhere. But where? And who killed him? He must have trusted the person he met at the cliff enough to divulge that secret, or he would still be alive. It only made sense to me that someone, perhaps in Newquay or at the hotel besides Rory Keene, knew Collin Newbury. I couldn't help but think that was precisely what our new acquaintance wanted us to believe.

Once we introduced ourselves to the police, we were afforded a more judicious freedom than that given the other patrons. And as sometimes happens where man's pride is concerned, when asked by Holmes if we could be of service in the investigation, we were curtly told by Penhale that we would be the first to be contacted if the investigation ran into any snags—their way of saying, no. With that, we were free to go about our business.

"Well, Watson, it seems celebrity has its certain privileges," he said with a feigned smugness as we walked back to our rooms. "I believe I shall make that bee symposium, after all,"

"With all that has happened?" I asked. "Are you not going to help Mr. Keene as you said you would?"

"I shall do both. There will be plenty of local enthusiasts at the symposium. I shall gather some *unauthorized* history of this house and see if that can shed any light on this little holiday mystery. In the meantime, stay with Mr. Keene and make sure he doesn't catch the eye of the constabulary for any reason. See what else you may be able to glean from him, keeping in mind that he may not have been completely truthful in what he has told us. Keep your friends close, Watson."

"And your enemies closer," I finished.

"I do not know that he is an enemy, but that is a reality which, when not correctly established, has been known to be fatal. It's best to keep him close at hand until I know for certain his word is true." He turned to go into his room then swung back around animatedly. "Oh yes," he added, "and if possible, speak to the manager about employees. I would be most curious to know if by chance Newbury knew anyone who worked here. We shall convene later this afternoon when I return, compare notes, and develop a plan of action from there."

There have always been times in the past where some seeming innocuous diversion from the case-proper served more in the development of a theory than any perceived lack of initiative on the part of Holmes, such as taking in the opera then promptly closing the infamous Marquess of Westminster diamond case. To that end, I no longer questioned my friend when he seemed to lose interest in our prey when it seemed we most needed to hunt. I, for my part, just shook my head in agreement, and Sherlock Holmes disappeared into his room to change into his beekeeper's outfit.

Within the hour, dressed in his bulky white uniform, his netted hat tucked under his arm, Holmes was in a taxi and on his way into Newquay, leaving Mr. Keene in my, what I had hoped, capable hands.

I waited by the front desk while the rest of the interviews took place. Shortly, the manager found his way to my spot.

"I am truly sorry, Doctor Watson, that you and Mr. Holmes couldn't even come on holiday without leaving this dreadful business of murder behind," said he in earnest.

I shrugged in a desultory way. "When you have been friends with Sherlock Holmes for as long as I have, these events take on the expectancy of afternoon tea."

He offered his hand, and we shook. "I haven't formally introduced myself. I am Willoughby Jones. I have been the manager at this hotel since its inception, and even being this close to Folly's End, no one has ever gone over the edge until today."

Remembering what Holmes had told me, I endeavored to start my own little investigation while he was off attending his bees. "What can you tell me about Mr. Newbury?" I asked.

The man gave a shrug of his shoulders. "If you've been around Newbury for more than five minutes, that's all you need to know about him. He was a horrible peddler, selling horrible clothing, and he seemed to rub just about everyone the wrong way."

"Yes, we had the misfortune of his sales pitch on the train from London. And he seemed to, as you say, rub your tour guide the wrong way yesterday afternoon."

Mr. Jones nodded his knowledge of the affair with irritation. "Yes, Mr. Vigus, the tour guide, bemoaned the constant rebarbative blather from Mr. Newbury. Apparently, he also had the audacity to correct him on some minor account of history."

I cleared my throat with no small amount of embarrassment. "The blathering was certainly coming from Newbury, but the correction came from Sherlock Holmes."

It was Mr. Jones's turn for his cheeks to redden. "I must have misunderstood. My apologies. No offense to Mr. Holmes."

"None taken, I assure you," I replied, knowing that peoples' feelings never got in the way of truth when it came to my friend.

"Truth be told," he went on, "Newbury, ruffled quite a few feathers at dinner last night, as well. His constant nuisance in interrupting people at their meals got to be too much, and I had to ask him to please take his seat for dinner or leave the restaurant."

"This must have been after our dinner."

"Yes, he was down late with about fifteen other guests, around half-nine, I think."

"I would not feel so bad for the man if he could in fact sell one of his suits. Do you know if he had any success?"

Jones shook his head. "From what I saw, he was rebuffed in no uncertain terms on every occasion. Yet it never seemed to bother the man."

As much as I would have liked to tell Jones that Newbury was a rich man whether he sold a suit or not, I kept that information close to my vest.

Finally, the man said, "I had entertained the hope that he would tire of coming here and move on to other hotels, maybe stay in Newquay. They have a fine hotel there. But for whatever reason, despite his lack of success here, he continued to fancy Kerrek House when he came to Cornwall."

I was surprised by that statement and strived to get clarification. "So, this was not Newbury's first time at Kerrek House?"

"Heavens no. This would make his fourth stay in the last year. I only know this because his presence here is never without its struggles."

"His peddling?"

"Yes."

"Has he made any acquaintances here? Anyone he has befriended or befriended him?"

"I am sure we all know him by now, but I doubt anyone here would consider him more than an annoyance, surely not a friend, but he does seem to try hard with the ladies on occasion. It might be that, with their comforting dispositions, that someone here might have taken pity on the man." He ended that statement with a curt chuckle. "But I highly doubt it."

It was at this point that I saw young Mr. Keene appear from the restaurant. We gave each other a telling look, and I thanked Mr. Jones for his time and followed Keene up to his room.

Once inside, he took a seat on his bed while I sat on the chair at his writing desk.

"So, all went well with the interview?" I asked.

He nodded. "They asked the standard fare—where was I from, why was I here, how long was I staying, did I know Mr., Newbury. I have to assume they will check us all out and soon enough they will know I was lying about knowing him."

"With as many people as they will have to go through," I assured him, "it will be some time before they get to you. Hopefully, by then this matter will be well in hand."

"Well, I would wager they go through the men first, since they could scarcely believe a woman would have the skill with a bow and arrow to strike a man through the back at such a distance. I don't think, Dr. Watson, that I have as much time as you might expect."

"What were your directives?" I asked.

Pushing back his hair, he said frustratedly, "We are to remain inside the hotel. In our rooms, in the restaurant, in the library, they didn't care, but we were under no circumstances to be outside until this matter is resolved."

"Rest assured, even though he is not here, I know Sherlock Holmes, and he will not let this go until the blackguard is in the docks."

"Holmes is not here? Where is he?"

I did not wish to aggravate Keene unduly, so I said, "We have been given a bit of a free reign, so Holmes went into Newquay to follow some theories of *interest* there."

Keene gave me a resentful glance.

"Trust me, Mr. Keene, Holmes has his methods, and it does no good to question them. The murderer will be found."

He replied, "I will not lose any sleep that the man is dead. I only wish to restore our good name and get a bit of retribution for my sister. Now, it seems, my hopes for either will not be seen through."

I endeavoured to keep Keene's spirits up and fulfill the expectations Holmes placed upon me before he left. I asked, "Did you happen to see anyone either on the train or perhaps here that looked familiar to you?"

Keene thought a moment then shook his head, "No, why?"

"Well, he either had an accomplice besides your sister, or he told someone else about the money. He would not have been killed had he been the only one with the knowledge of the money's location. So, either he came with someone, in which case, since you've been following him for some time, you might have seen someone you recognize, or he had a confidant here at the hotel or nearby. I was told that he had stayed here on other occasions."

"I assure you he has not been here in the time that I have been following him," Keene replied steadfastly. "This man was shrewd, confident, and patient," he went on in a tone of almost undesirable awe. "He knew if he just waited for his moment, he could just disappear with all that money. He needed to be sure there was no hint that he was under any investigation. He had waited forbearingly for a year. That is a lifetime to be without when you know riches are at your fingertips. His will was made of iron. But alas, that unbridled tongue of his was his downfall."

The young man looked around the room and sighed. "So, we just sit here until Mr. Holmes comes back?"

I wanted to stay stagnant as much as he did and felt I was wasting time doing nothing. I rose and said, "No, I feel we need to do something. I do not want my friend to come back without some kind of a breakthrough and his faith in me shall have been wasted."

"By Jove, I'm all for that. Where shall we go? What shall we do?"

"I am not sure precisely why, but my inclination is to go back up to the observation room at the top of the hotel. From there you can see off in any direction. I feel as though I've been missing something up there, and it has been gnawing at me for some time."

"I've not been there myself. Lead the way."

"We have to be careful," I said as we left his room. "To get there is beyond normal guest access unless we are on a tour of the manor house. I am sure Mr. Jones, the manager, would give me access, but I cannot say the same for the constabulary, should they be skulking about."

"I've been using subterfuge for some time, now. It is nothing new to me."

When we descended the great Jade staircase the double glass doors were to our front, and several uniformed men were sentried either at the door or in the gravel drive making conversation. To our left, Mr. Jones, wearing a critical expression, was speaking in hushed tones to the front receptionist, and to our right several guests were either sitting at the pub or the tables in the restaurant, all with the same worried look and same intense divulgences as the manager.

"It is this way," said I, as we left the open area of the vestibule and made our way around to the great wall of weapons. I was going to point out where the longbow had been taken when we stopped in our tracks. Standing in front of the door at the end was a tall, thin constable. He hadn't yet noticed us, for he was playing with what appeared to be a loose button on his uniform.

We hid ourselves around the corner near one of the suits of armour as we weighed our options.

"Should we just go up and tell the constable to let us through?" Keene asked. "You are the articulator of the great Sherlock Holmes. Surely, they will let you through."

"Possibly, but under no circumstances am I to throw any light in your direction with regards to the police. Holmes wants you to stay as unremarkable and unnoticed until his return."

"Surely, my being with you can only help my cause."

"One thing you might find curious about our professional counterparts is that many who only know Sherlock Holmes by name do not wish for his intrusion into their investigations. Those who know him intimately will come to him with no pretense. We all want the same outcome—the guilty behind bars, but career narcissism has let many a man go free when Holmes's overtures are rebuffed."

Keene gave me a turned brow. "They refused his help?"

"It has happened more than you might think."

We both thought a moment in silence. Finally, Keene smiled and said, "I have an idea. Stay here. I will draw him away from the door."

Before I could object, he was out in the middle of the hall acting as though he were drunk.

"Hey," said the constable. "Hey! You can't be down here. You need to stay back in the hotel section of the property."

Staggering, Keene replied in a slur, "I—I'm looking for the loo. The a-ale's goin' right through me."

With that, he fell onto the floor.

"A little help h-here."

"Bloody hell," replied the annoyed constable. "It's barely passed nine, and you're already bladdered."

He helped Keene to his feet.

"Can you at l-least get me to the loo? I won't be a bother after that. I'll go t-to me room and sleep this bugger off."

"Alright, alright. I think it's down this way."

As he helped Keene along, I took the opportunity to sneak my way down the hall and into the residential area. It was empty. I made my way up to Josephine's Room then up the stairs to the observation room. The day was a bright and beautiful one. The fog had completely dissipated, but the winds coming off the Atlantic were still robust.

I was unsure what I was looking for but felt I was missing something right in front of me. The gravel drive meandered off into the distance. The garden stretched out to the east and south for a few hundred yards, the tops of arborvitae and yews swirling in the breezes not rebuffed by the pine windbreak.

And there it was hiding in plain sight. The abandoned Wheal Kerrek. The old tin mine. I had been so focused on the house proper for the whereabouts of the money that it had never occurred to me until just now that it might just be somewhere on the property. The abandoned tin mine would make the perfect spot to hide ten-thousand pounds.

Rejuvenated at the thought, I ran back down the stairs. In Josephine's Room, something caught my eye which stopped me in my tracks. I stared up at the large tapestry of the property. Something I had never noticed before now stood out painfully obvious. The tapestry showed all the veins of the mine spidering out from Wheal Kerrek to the surrounding area. One of those veins ran straight from the mine to Kerrek House.

I needed to find out where that tunnel was and knew precisely the person to ask.

Slowly opening the door back out into the great hall of weapons, I had hoped and so it was granted that the guard was not yet back at his post. It seemed that Mr. Keene was an admirable diversionist.

I began in haste back down the hall when the constable reappeared from around the corner ahead of me. I did the only thing I could think to do—I turned and began to examine the implements on the wall.

"Say, you cannot be down here," said the constable.

"My apologies," I replied. "I was bored, and, having remembered this impressive display from a tour of the house last night, thought I would come down and take in the exhibit with a more leisurely eye. I had no idea that this area was off-limits."

He motioned for me to leave. "I'm afraid so, sir, so please keep yourself confined to the front of the hotel or your room."

I nodded acquiescence and removed myself. I found Keene sitting on the staircase awaiting my return.

"Well?" he asked.

"Come with me. I think I might have found something."

I approached the manager, who was still at the front desk with the receptionist, with Rory Keene in tow.

"Mr. Jones, I was wondering if you happened to know if that tapestry in Josephine's Room is a true rendering of Wheal Kerrek and its various tunnels?"

Nodding, the man replied, "Yes, it is. Several tunnels have collapsed over the years, but that tapestry is an accurate depiction of all the working veins of Wheal Kerrek when it was made in 1763."

"Then there is a tunnel that runs under Kerrek House?"

"Under, no. It ends at the east end near the kitchen."

"Is it accessible?" I asked.

He thought for a moment. "Not without some trouble. That part of the lower portion of Kerrek House was converted to a wine cellar. I believe there are wine racks in front of the door that leads to that vein. It hasn't been used in over a hundred years. I'm not even sure the door could be opened if you could get to it."

With a hopeful vigor, I said, "Please take us there."

"Us?" he asked looking around. "I don't believe Mr. Holmes is back yet from Newquay."

"Mr. Keene is with me. I take full responsibility for him."

Jones shrugged. "Whatever you say, doctor."

He led us down some service stairs at the back of the restaurant which ended in a large room filled with ovens and counters with a myriad of cooking utensils hanging from the ceiling. Several workers were busily going about their day preparing dishes of all sorts.

"Would anyone have been down here cooking at six this morning?" I asked.

Jones replied, "No. Our food staff normally do not start preparing for the day until 7:00 for an 8:30 breakfast unless we are at full occupancy, which we are not."

At the far end of the kitchen was a small doorway on the right and wide archway with a dark hallway that lay beyond on the left.

"This way, gentlemen," said Jones going under the archway. We found ourselves in a long, cool, dark corridor that gradually opened into a small, open area with curved walls and ceiling. Racks of wine bottles lined the walls on three sides.

He turned on an electric light switch, bathing the area in a sour yellow hue. Pointing, Jones said, "The door to the tunnel is on the other side of those far wine racks, but as I said, I'm not even sure…" His voice trailed off for he saw what was very obvious to all: one of the wine racks had been pulled forward. There were scratches on the floor and disturbances in the dust in an arcing pattern left when the heavy wine rack was pulled forward. It had been partially pushed back into place but was still slightly ajar.

"By Jove, you were right, Doctor Watson!" exclaimed Keene. "Someone has gone into the tunnel."

Jones asked, "Do you think the murderer escaped by this route? I can hardly believe it myself."

"It seems the evidence is pointing in that direction," I replied. "Can you currently account for every guest at the hotel?"

"I cannot," he replied. "Most, I assume, went back to their rooms. Some are in the restaurant and some in the library."

Is there another way to this spot besides going through the kitchen?"

Jones replied forlornly, "There is. It is a servant's entrance. It was that doorway to the right of the archway. You can gain access to it at the end of the first-floor hallway in the east wing."

Keened interjected, "And the guests were interviewed first. All the staff would have still been in the restaurant, waiting their turn, so no one would have been downstairs to see the scoundrel leave."

I turned and faced Jones directly. "Do you have access to any lanterns?"

"Yes."

"Can you procure one, please."

"You aren't going in there, are you?"

"What would you have me do?"

"Tell the police."

"I will leave you to your conscience. In the meantime, we must make haste to find this blackguard. There is more to this murder than you are privy to Jones, and no time can be wasted."

Jones ran back down the hall while Keene pulled out the wine rack to make room to open the door.

"It is a bit heavy, but I don't think it entirely impossible that the murderer could have pulled the rack back as he closed the door."

Using my experience with untold cases with Holmes and the methods he used, I disagreed. "Sometimes, the simplest answers are the best ones. It is more probable that he or she had help, and it was the person on this side of the wine rack that pushed it back in place."

"Since it wasn't completely pushed back," Keened offered, "Then maybe the person was not strong enough to push it completely back against the door."

"Or they were interrupted. As my friend would say, *we need more data.*"

Jones returned with a lantern, already lit. "We keep lanterns strategically placed throughout the hotel in case of a power failure. There are several in the kitchen."

He handed it to me.

"Thank you," said I.

"I feel it my duty to inform the constables of this discovery," Jones replied.

"Do as you see fit," I said. "I do not know how long we shall be in here. Should Sherlock Holmes return before us, let him know what we've discovered the second he steps foot into the hotel."

"I shall."

By this time, Keene had pulled back the wine rack enough to open the old door with a whining screech to the point that we could both squeeze through sideways.

"Are you ready, Dr. Watson?" he asked.

I nodded. "Let us see if we can find that murderer."

"Let's see if we can find that ten thousand pounds," Keene replied dryly.

I saw Jones's countenance register an unexpected shock as we disappeared behind the door. I heard him exclaim, "Wait, what? What ten-thousand pounds?"

. . . . .

We made our way cautiously down the tunnel. Our shadows, distorted with jagged lines from ancient, pick-axe-marked walls, followed clumsily along. I thought perhaps our presence would echo in the surrounding area, but the walls only seemed to deaden our footfalls.

"How far does this tunnel go?" Keene whispered to me.

Recalling the tapestry, I did my best at using recollection, trying to put into practice what Holmes and I had discussed on the train ride to Cornwall. "I believe it will go on for a few hundred yards before it reaches the main tunnel. That will take you right to the entrance to Wheal Kerrek at the edge of the cliff. There are four tunnels that branch off this one, two on either side, but not until we get closer to the main tunnel. From there, a multitude of smaller veins branch off."

I could hear Holmes's sarcastic *"Bravo, Watson! Except..."* in my ears for I was sure that I was wrong in my remembrance on some point.

After a minute or two, I could see the vein opening a few hundred feet ahead, which probably meant we were coming upon the other branches of the tunnel. There was something odd as I squinted into the inky spaces beyond my lanternlight. It seemed something was moving.

I held out my hand for Keene to stop.

"Do you see something?" he asked.

"Possibly. I am going to douse my light. Do you see it down there, now?" I asked pointing.

Keene squinted. "Yes, what is it?" He looked harder. "It's light."

"Yes," I replied. "We need the element of surprise, so we shall go blind from here." I turned off my lantern and placed it on the ground. The two of us proceeded in darkness from there with only the faint glow of light ahead of us as a marker to our destination.

We finally reached the open area, and I had been correct—the light was coming from here. Its brilliance was just enough to illuminate our surroundings. We were now in a large carved-out section with a ten-foot ceiling and was twice that in width. Ahead of us the tunnel stretched into an inky darkness. There were two smaller veins hewn into the right wall that were just high enough for anyone under six feet tall walk without crouching. The light was emanating through the second of those veins.

As we crept past the first vein, I noticed that at about thirty feet in there was an opening, connecting the two tunnels. There, at that opening, crouching, was a large man. He looked thick in the shadows, formidable, but his entirety was obscured in darkness. I could not tell, exactly, but it looked as though he was facing away from us. I could see no more in the gloom, other than he seemed hunched over, possibly inspecting the ground at his feet.

Silently, I pointed at the figure to Keene, and he acknowledged seeing the person, as well. "Our murderer," he whispered.

Suddenly, in the blink of an eye, the figure was no longer in his spot. I had just looked away for a moment to acknowledge Keene, and when I looked back the hunched figure was no longer there. "Where did he go?" I asked.

"I didn't see him get up," Keene said softly. "I can barely see my hand before my face, and this gloom can be disorienting. Do you think he went back into the other tunnel?"

"Let's find out," I replied.

We inched over to the second tunnel. I stealthily peered around the rock wall. The tunnel curved to the left, and the light was radiating from somewhere out of my line of sight. I could also hear what sounded like digging in the distance.

Shortly, Keene was by my side. "I think we need to go into that other tunnel to get a clearer picture of what he is up to," I said.

"I think you are correct. I don't think the person knows exactly where the money is hidden. I think they are digging helter-skelter in different areas trying to find the right spot."

"That may have been the reason for Newbury's murder," I murmured. He would not give up its exact location. The killer might be digging in here for weeks before finding the money."

We then retreated quietly and made our way down the first tunnel. About ten feet from the opening between the two small tunnels where we had seen the shadowed rogue, in absolute darkness, Keene lost his balance behind me. The hard scuffling of his feet made me think he had tripped and fallen.

"Careful," I whispered over my shoulder.

There was no reply.

"Keene?" I reached out into the darkness at nothing. He was gone.

My only thought was he must have decided to do something I had worried was never far from his thoughts: mete out justice for his dead sister.

I made my way as fast and as quietly as I could to the spot where I could observe the curved part of the second tunnel, half-expecting to see Keene running wild-eyed at Newbury's and his sister's—at least in his eyes—murderer. Stealth would no doubt be broken momentarily, and I had to ready myself for that inevitability, hoping against hope that the worst we would encounter was a spade and not a revolver.

Without warning, a large, skeletal hand wrapped around my mouth, preventing an exclamation that most assuredly would have given me up, and I found myself being pulled back into the darkness of another tunnel I knew nothing about.

"Watson!" came a harsh whisper. "Watson, it's Holmes. I shall take my hand from around your mouth. Please do me the favor of not giving up our position."

He slowly moved his hand away.

"Holmes, what in blazes are you doing here?" I whispered however hard it may have been to keep from remonstrating him at the top of my lungs.

"A conversation for another time," he replied softly. "Right now, we need to catch our thief."

"Mr. Keene was with me. I fear he has abdicated to get to that money and restore his family name."

"Never fear, Doctor Watson," came a whispered reply from the darkness next to me. "Mr. Holmes corralled me first."

"I am waiting for the recovery of the money before I close in," said Holmes.

"I hope he finds it soon," said I. "I fear Mr. Jones has told the constabulary and soon the tunnels will be full of police."

"I am fine with that," replied Keene. "He is a murderer and thief, and he belongs in the same place Newbury would have gone. My retribution will be requited with the restoration of the money and hopefully the dignity of the Keene name."

"I think you will be happy on all accounts," said Holmes. "Come, let us get our man. But we must be careful. He has a weapon."

As we spoke, the hue of the light two tunnels away changed. It was lessening.

Holmes hurried across the tunnel with myself and Keene at his back. He looked into the other tunnel and found it empty. "He must have found the money. Hurry! We must catch him before he can escape entirely."

The three of us hurried down the tunnel to the larger vein that stretched into the distance to Kerrek House. A small but growing light emitted from the far end.

"Here come our comrades," said Holmes. "Come. This way. No doubt he will try to make his getaway by the main entrance."

As we raced towards the main vein of Wheal Kerrek, the inky blackness around us gave way to a growing illumination. It was here that I could see Holmes in his beekeeper's outfit. That was why he looked so brutish amongst the shadows.

Once at the junction, to our left roughly one hundred feet, was a large opening to the cliff and the ocean beyond. A rotted railing surrounded a small landing. An old tarpaulin covered in untold years of dirt and muck lay half-in, half-out of the entrance, partially covering the dilapidated landing. Stairs that looked equally suspect ran up to the right, no doubt to the skeletal remains of the mining structure itself.

Just short of the opening was a man carrying a large, stained bag of money. There was something familiar about him. Something about the hair, the clothes…the suit.

"Mr. Newbury!" Holmes called out. "You may as well stop there. There is no way you can get away from me."

When he turned, he pointed a pistol in our direction. "No further," he said. "It isn't exactly my nature, but I am not averse to using this if pushed."

"Come, come," my friend said. "There are a handful of constables making their way down the tunnel from Kerrek House as we speak, and no doubt there will be a similar number above shortly. You do not have the ammunition to kill us all, but it takes only one for which to hang. Right now, robbery is all you are on the dock for."

Newbury, wild-eyed, backed up a step but still held the pistol at us.

"You have nowhere else to go," said Holmes. "Let us end this game without any dramatics."

"It doesn't matter, does it? I owe debts that I cannot repay without this money. And the arms of those gentlemen have a long reach, sir. A prison sentence is as good as a death sentence, so I cannot end this game the way you wish it to end."

"So, it was you who owed the money and not your brother," offered Keene angrily.

Newbury gave Keene a quizzical eye. "Do I know you, sir? How did you know that?"

"Esme was my sister."

He nodded knowingly. "You must be Rory. She spoke of you often."

By this time, a group of six constables were at our backs. Holmes motioned for them to stand down.

"She loved you almost as much as she loved me," Newbury said, as a man almost in the throes of jealousy.

"And you used her, you scum! You poisoned her mind to this robbery by feigning a love that did not exist."

Tears began to well in Newbury's eyes. His next words held bitter notes. "Do you think you are the only one on earth capable of loving someone like Esme? You are wrong, sir, I loved her like no other. I knew about her fits and cared not a tittle about them. In fact, her need of me drew me all the closer to her. I've seen the seizures first-hand. I held her as she shook, stroked her hair, kissed her cheek until the fit had passed. She would tell me that some seemed to last forever, but when I was there to comfort her, they were over in minutes. Strange as it may sound, I had found my calling, and I would have done anything for her. I wanted, no *needed* to take care of her. It seemed to be the only thing in life I was any good at."

"Then why get her involved in all of this?" Keene retorted.

Holmes, hands raised in submission, slowly walked in Newbury's direction. "Come. I am not armed, and you are. Let us talk this out. I am submitting myself to you so we can end this peacefully."

Holmes halved the distance between them before Newbury even seemed to notice him. He waved the pistol forcefully at Holmes, which made him stop.

Giving his attention back to Keene, with whom he seemed more interested in conversing asked, "Don't you see? She was a willing participant. She seemed to know instinctively that we were made for each other. My only purpose in life, I had come to realize, was to take care of her. But my past was catching up to me. I owed dark people in dark places a lot of money. I concocted the story about my brother's debts, for I was embarrassed as to my faults and the depths to which they had thrown me. Out of desperation and her love for me, it was Esme who came up with this plan, far-fetched as it was. It was a reach, but it could work. I told my debtors if they would but wait one year, I would pay double what I owed. That would give me time to throw off any investigations into the missing money. They were keen on doubling their money so they agreed, knowing how this would end if I did not fulfill my obligation. They told me I would be followed wherever I went so trying to flee the country would only end badly for me. I agreed to whatever they demanded, and the die was cast. Esme and I were cautiously optimistic that this could wipe the slate clean, so to speak, and we could start over."

"Why here?" Holmes asked.

"When I was a lad, we had family in Newquay we visited every summer. I knew about Folly's End and Wheal Kerrek and figured the old mine was the perfect place to hide it. That was where we were headed before the accident. We took to the hills to get to Par, then from there, we would fetch a carriage to Newquay, for we knew the train stations would be watched." He shrugged in resignation. "We did not even get to Par before she fell from the rock and all was lost."

Holmes was slowly eclipsing the distance between the two as he continued to question Newbury, who seemed lost in his thoughts at the remembrance of that day a year ago.

"That was quite the taken chance, showing yourself back at the bank," Holmes went on.

"I then read in the paper that Esme had died in police custody before she named her accomplice, and it broke my heart. But I also knew that they now had no clue about me. I did the only thing I could think to do—I hid the money here, returned to St. Austell and went back to work, feigning illness as a way to further throw off my pursuers. I figured if I were so bold as to return to work that maybe they would think it couldn't be me. I worked another month then left it to sell suits until I felt safe enough to retrieve the money."

Keene did not seem satisfied with Newbury's dissertation. "If you loved her, then why did you leave her there in that field injured while you got clean away with the money?"

Suddenly, a voice cried out from above, "You are now surrounded. You may as well give it up." The second group of constables had arrived, effectively cutting off Newbury's only route of escape.

Keeping his pistol pointing at us, Newbury quickly craned his neck back and peered up the stairs. He moaned slightly but recovered himself as he fixed his stare squarely back to us. "At that point," he went on, "I knew the jig was up. I sat in the grass with her for a time, holding her. Right then, I was prepared to give up along with her. But she wouldn't have any of it. It was then that she confided in me that she knew—though I still do not know how—it was my debts and not my brother's for which the money was to be used. She begged me, tears in her eyes, to leave, take the money and pay the debts. She would say it was a stranger who'd robbed the bank and took her hostage. She would cast no nets of culpability in my direction."

"Yet, you showed by leaving where your loyalties truly lay," said Holmes as he took a few more tentative steps towards Newbury and stopped. "And the poor girl died for her trouble."

Backing up slowly, his pistol beginning to shake, Newbury said, "And I've had to live with that knowledge from that day to this. Do you not think had I known she was to have a seizure in the custody of the police that I would not have gladly given back the money to hold her one more time? Look into her eyes and tell her all would be well one more time?"

He pointed the pistol up the stairs as he backed against the railing then pointed it back at Holmes, who by now was only about fifteen feet from Newbury. "Who are you?" he asked my friend as if noticing him for the first time. "You don't have the look of the constabulary. In fact," he said in obvious reference to Holmes's attire, "I'm not quite certain what you have the look of."

I would have found the comment amusing had the situation not been so dire.

"I am Sherlock Holmes."

"Of course, you are," he replied in lamented sarcasm. "Why should my luck change now?"

The man's shoulders slumped in dejection.

Holmes began his slow, cautious trek to close the remaining distance between them, hands stretched in a calming manner. "It does not seem that you truly have murderous intent, on me or anyone here. Let us end this in a civilized manner. We can keep you safe while you serve your sentence, and you may still be young enough to enjoy some of your life upon your release."

He ignored Holmes, now, and only peered upon Keene, regret in his eyes. "Whatever else you may think of me, rest assured, you were not the only one who loved Esme—whose job it was to look out for her. It seems we've both failed on that account."

Newbury paused for a moment, in seeming reflection as to whether he would fight for his freedom or give up. He made his choice when, head sunk into his chest despondently, he dropped the pistol and bag at his feet.

"Good man," said Holmes as he closed the remaining distance between them.

Suddenly, he looked up, tears streaming down his ruddy cheeks, "I will be sure to let Esme know that her brother was still looking out for her, even in death."

With that, Newbury leaned back against the rotted railing, which quickly gave way. Holmes lunged at the man and grabbed at his lapel to try and reign him in, but in the attempt and with momentum pushing him forward, they both were gone in an instant, falling over the side of the landing.

There were several audible gasps, and I cried out, "Holmes!" as I raced to the rickety platform. I quickly crawled on my hands and knees to the edge and peered over the side. At first, all I could see was the twisted body of Newbury on the rocks below. I did not see Holmes. Had he fallen into the waves crashing nearby? "Holmes!" I cried out.

"You look but you do not observe," was the unlikely response. To my great surprise, Holmes was clutching a wooden brace under the landing that was still securely embedded into the side of the cliff out of my line of site. In one hand was the ripped lapel of Newbury's suit.

"Double stitching would have held, Watson," he replied dryly as he tossed the fabric from his hand for a firmer hold on the brace. "I would be greatly appreciative if you could extract me from this predicament before the entire platform gives way."

With help from two constables, we soon had Holmes back to the safety of the landing.

With a queer solemnity, he, Keene and I peered over the edge at the lifeless body on the rocky beach below.

"All this in the name of love," said I.

"We reap what we sow, Watson."

With that, we all turned and made our way back to Kerrek house while the constabulary tended to the gruesome task of recovering the body.

Once back in the safe confines of Kerrek House, we three sat at a table in the restaurant. Most of the hotel was down for lunch by then. Our robust adulterer, now alone, took a table next to ours and started eagerly eyeing the menu as we sipped on some well-deserved tea.

"So, tell me, Holmes," I started. "When did you know it was Newbury and how? I thought you were going to the bee symposium."

"And I was, Watson. But I had an epiphany while in the taxi. I had him drop me off at the end of the drive, and I made my way back to Wheal Kerrek to test my theory. Of course, I was correct."

"But we thought we were on the trail of Newbury's murderer, not Newbury himself. How did you know?"

Holmes lit a cigarette and inhaled with a satisfying air. "The first thing I found odd is the fact that only one person saw him killed."

"Two," I replied. "Me and a member of the staff."

"Quite right, quite right. Yet, I believe only *one* was supposed to truly witness it. You just happened to be in the right place at the right time."

"She was meant to witness his death? Why?"

"Patience, my dear fellow. You want to see the picture before the puzzle pieces are all in their rightful place. The next piece was given to me by our new friend, Mr. Keene."

He looked to one than the other of us. "What did I do?" he asked with astonishment.

"You mentioned only looking through two suits in his wardrobe when you were looking for clues as to the whereabouts of the money, yes?"

Thinking momentarily, Keene then replied, "That's right, Mr. Holmes. There were only two suits in his wardrobe. So?"

"You were not acquainted with this bit of information, young Mr. Keene, but Watson, you were. When he approached us on the train, he mentioned having three suits available to try on, plus the one he was wearing. That is four suits. There were no other clothes in his room but what was in his wardrobe, so, if he was wearing one, and two were there, where did the other one go?"

"Quite right," said I. "Those were not for sale—they were only product for show. And little help they did him. From what the manager told me when I asked, he tried mightily at dinner to get a sale but was rebuffed at every turn."

Holmes waved my statement off, whimsically, "Please, Watson, did you *really* feel the need to ask if he had sold any?"

"I was only trying to give the man the benefit of the doubt."

"Ever the optimist, my dear Watson." He took a sip of tea and refilled his cup. "The next link in the gruesome chain was when we made our way back up to the observation room."

"But you said yourself that was a fruitless task."

"I said nothing of the sort. I believe I said that going up there revealed more than you realized. Observe, do not just see, Watson. My guess is you remembered the tapestry and that was how you knew about the tunnel from the house to the mine."

"That is correct," I said with some satisfaction.

"But there was something up there that you missed. It is the tables on the train all over again."

After a long silence, I finally said in exasperation, "Will you just come out and say it, what did I miss?"

He gave one of his curt smiles, the kind that are there and gone in the blink of an eye. "Had you counted the mannequins you would have realized that there was one missing."

Putting it all together, I then said as I formed the events in my head, "So, Newbury planned this fake murder by dressing up a mannequin in one of his suits, setting it up by the overlook of Folly's End, and shooting it in the back with an arrow, the force of the impact taking it over the edge, so people would see what looked like Newbury falling to his death."

"But why?" asked Keene.

"Though he did not give us this information, my theory would be that he was planning this show for the individual tasked to be his shadow. If they thought he was dead, his debtors would be forced to call off the dogs. He then would be able to start fresh with all the money instead of only part, or perhaps none of it."

"A brilliant plan, I must admit," said I.

"Precisely, Watson. However, he needed a witness for this plan to work. That is where the crying woman comes in."

With that, Holmes looked up and, seeing a constable standing near the entranceway with a netted hat tucked under his arm, craning his head over the patrons, stood and waved him over.

"Ah, there you are, Mr. Holmes," he said as he approached. "I found this in the field when we were canvassing the area. I knew right away it belonged to you."

"Thank you, constable," he said, taking it and putting it on the table next to him. "While I have you here, I was hoping you could do me a service."

"If I can, surely, Mr. Holmes?"

"There was a young lady who was unfortunate to have thought she witnessed a murder, I do not know her name, but I am sure you can get it from the hotel manager."

"It was Miss Forrester, Mr. Holmes. She was the first person we talked to."

"Yes, do you happen to know where she is at the moment?"

"I am sure she is about somewhere. No one has left the premises."

"Thank you. Could you be so kind as to arrest her."

"Arrest her? For what reason?"

"She played a part in this little ruse. I am sure if you tell her that Newbury implicated her before his death, she will come clean."

"I will certainly pass this along to Chief Constable Penhale. He is due back any moment."

"Where did he fly off to?" I asked.

"He has been in Newquay arranging boats to go fetch the body at low tide. We sent word that the matter has been resolved, and we expect him back shortly."

"Wonderful, thank you," said Holmes.

When the constable left, he returned his attention to us. "That was the epiphany I had in the taxi."

"The woman?" asked Keene.

"No, that was elementary. If there was no one to see him fall…"

"If a tree falls in the woods, and no one is there to hear it, does it make a sound?"

"In a curiously roundabout way, yes, Mr. Keene. He needed a witness to see him fall. But one he could trust. He could not have just anyone or even a multitude of people witness it. That would greatly increase the chances of someone noticing a mannequin instead of an actual person. The particularly foggy morning only helped mask the charade. Oh, this was well-planned, well-planned indeed."

I contemplated Holmes's proposition for a moment. "But she could have been an unwitting accomplice," I finally replied after some thought. "If he knew that she would be preparing for breakfast and opening up curtains, he could have timed the stunt for her to be witness to it. He has been here a few times before. Certainly, he knew their routine."

"Capital, Watson! A well-contrived rebuttal. That was data I was not aware of but had expected, nonetheless. You are correct on all but one aspect. No one but she was up preparing for breakfast at 6 a.m. Certainly, it does not take two-and-half hours to prepare for breakfast in a hotel that holds roughly sixty guests and is not at capacity. No, I believe he befriended her and manipulated her, much the same way he did Miss Keene. In the end, these women were nothing more than pawns to Newbury, regardless of his professed affections to at least one of them. I would have had more sympathy for the man had he just paid his debts like a gentleman."

"Yet, you risked your life to save his," I reminded.

"I saw where the situation was headed, my dear fellow. I very much dislike self-executed castigation. I prefer physical transgressions be paid with physical judgment. The one to come is above my station."

"Do you think it was her footprints in the wet grass we saw along with his? Miss Forrester's, I mean?"

"No, both sets were his, one setting up his doppelganger and one as he left to set up for his target practice."

"And all this was happening while I was upstairs rooting through his room?" Keene asked.

"You missed a lot," said I.

Holmes put out his cigarette and drank down the rest of what was surely by now cold tea. "Now, gentlemen, we come to the *plat de resistance.* I had all these pieces and knew not what to do with them, at first. How slow-witted I have been today. I can only blame my preoccupation with the bee symposium. But in the taxi, I realized that at low tide, when they recovered the body, the police would know they had been played. That meant Newbury only had until 11:30 this morning to get the money and leave the area before everyone would know he was still alive. All this came to me as I stared out the window at the dilapidated Wheal Kerrek in the distance. Then, the tapestry came to me, and the tunnel, then I knew in an instant where Newbury was."

"And now, here we sit," I replied.

"Not quite the ending I had hoped for," lamented Rory Keene. "I had thought without any doubts whatsoever that Newbury had only been using my sister as some sort of scapegoat so he could make off with the money. It had never occurred to me that he might truly have feelings for my sister."

"In my experience," I offered sincerely, glancing over at Holmes, "what one might call a handicap and something detrimental to the human condition only serves to make them a more special human being. Some people have a propensity to see that, many do not."

Though the sentiment was offered indirectly to Holmes, he had paid no mind to the remark. Instead, he wore a determined look as he scrutinized the plump philanderer at the table next to us with his face in the menu.

Holmes at last stood and regarded us once more. "Now that this little affair has been handled, I am off to see if I can still get a glimpse of the rare cuckoo bee before it is too late."

"Well, I hope you can find some solace in what is left of the symposium. It is too bad that this has taken you away from the reason for your visit to Cornwall."

With a laugh and a wave of his hand my friend replied, "Nonsense, Watson. I couldn't have asked for a better holiday."

Holmes grabbed his hat and tucked it up under his arm. But before he left, he tapped at the menu of stranger from the train beside us. "Give your masters a message from me. Tell them Mr. Newbury is dead, and the police have recovered the stolen money. You shall not collect a penny of the debt."

Without looking at him, the man asked, "And who should I say this message is from?"

"Tell them they can thank this misfortune on Sherlock Holmes."

Once Holmes left the restaurant, the man got up himself and followed suit.

"How on earth did Holmes know that was Newbury's tail?" Keene asked taken aback.

All I could do was shrug. "What happened to the lost settlement at Roanoke? Is there life on other planets? Will anyone ever decipher the Riemann Hypothesis? Count Sherlock Holmes's abilities among the questions in life that may never be answered."

The End

Elementary

It was a cold, wet, and windswept Saturday evening nearing the Ides of March. The beginning of 1899 had seen some of the coldest and most inclement weather since that dreadful 'year without a summer', which was the impetus for author Mary Shelley's infamous tale *Frankenstein*, at the pistol shot of the century. With but a few days of respite as the exception, the weather had been abnormally chilled and wet for the better part of a month that usually heralded in Spring with blooming flowers and a thawing sun. The temperatures as of late hovered just enough above freezing to keep the precipitation in liquid form, but Winter, it seemed, had no intention of letting the warmer months get a foothold in London. In fact, it was of sufficient brutality that my old war wound, which often gave me fits in the extremes of weather, was causing me some discomfort. I did my best to ignore it by reading the paper, while Holmes plucked ruefully at his violin. With my malaise and his boredom, it made for a peculiarly restless atmosphere—with an irritatingly out-of-tune E string intermittently thrown in.

So, it was with much enthusiasm that we both rose from our chairs when there came the familiar knock at the door downstairs.

"I do hope it is good news, Watson," Holmes declared. "I am at my wits' end in these cold and wet doldrums. Perhaps it is Lestrade in need of our help."

Stretching my aches as I folded the paper and placed it on the sideboard, I replied, "So you wish someone ill all for the sake of relieving your boredom?"

My friend shot me a feigned, hurtful look. "Don't be silly, Watson. I would settle for a simple blackmail, a tidy, little government conspiracy…a cipher. An unsharpened ax cannot chop wood."

As we heard the footsteps upon the floorboards Holmes perked an ear. "Those are the unmistakable strides of our compatriot from Scotland Yard. Things are indeed looking up."

Holmes ran to the door and opened it just as Lestrade was about to knock. He was wet in his waterproof and looked miserable.

"Ah, Lestrade, we thought it you coming up the stairs." He ushered the man in with a long sweep of his bow. "A brandy? It is a night not fit for man nor beast."

Lestrade nodded a terse, yes, to me as I retrieved the glasses and brandy. "Yet, here I am," he replied glumly then sneezed. His skin was grey, his cheeks sunk into his face, and the man had dark circles about his eyes as though he hadn't slept in days.

"You look unwell," said I, as I poured the drinks.

"A cold that seems to have taken to me like a lost dog."

"Shall I prepare you something for it?"

He waved the statement off. "I have tried every bloody remedy out there with no results. And let me tell you, anyone with any amount of hair on his chest would be a fool to try porous plaster. Oh, application is the easy part. There is nothing in the instructions, however, to warn you of the hellish ordeal of taking it off if left to dry! No, this blasted thing will leave me when it's good and ready. I am quite tired of the fight."

Holmes grinned cheekily but made no comment. He tossed his violin and bow onto a side table and offered Lestrade a seat by the fire, which he gladly took after he removed his coat and placed it on a hook on the mantle to dry out.

I gave us each a glass of brandy, and we sat down, anxious to hear what conundrum had brought Lestrade to us.

Holmes gave the inspector a querying look. "So, what brings you to our digs on a dreary, despicable night like this?"

Lestrade retrieved a handkerchief from his pocket and blew his nose before beginning. "There's been a murder not too far from here. A professor from City of London University over in Northampton Square was killed in his flat. He and his wife live a few streets away from the university on Paget. According to the missus, she was knitting in bed, which is her custom, while the husband, a Mr. Harold Austin, was tinkering around with chemicals in a self-made laboratory he has in the loft above the flat. The wife said she heard what she thought was an explosion upstairs. She roused herself to investigate and was bowled over by an unknown man as she rounded the corner to the steps leading up to the loft. Before she could regain herself, he had bounded the entrance stairs and ran out the front door."

Holmes interrupted, "She did not know who it was with whom she collided?"

"She says not. Apparently, he entertains students frequently in his laboratory, and she pays no mind to their comings or goings, which according to her, they do at all hours. She is certain, though, that when she retired for the evening, he was alone. At her husband's request, she leaves the door unlocked for certain students to pop in, and he locks up before retiring himself." He took a robust swallow of brandy then went on, "At any rate, after recovering herself, she looked in on her husband. She found him slumped over in his chair where he'd been writing out formulas of some sort. He had a single gunshot wound in his back. By the time she had rushed to his side he was dead."

Holmes, who had thusly locked his fingers together as he listened unfurled his index fingers and began tapping them together impatiently. "That sounds rather straightforward, Lestrade. Surely, this is something well within your realm of reasoning to resolve. What need of us do you have?"

The veiled sarcasm was not lost on the inspector, and he replied irascibly, "Because chemistry was not one of my academic strongpoints, if you must know, Holmes! I know you have a fondness for that sort of muckety-muck and decided you might be of help in some capacity as it may relate to his death."

"He was a chemist," my friend replied, "yet, it seems to me physics played the larger part in the man's demise. How can my erudition help in solving this little affair?"

Lestrade gulped down the rest of the brandy and held it out to me for a refill, which I obliged. He then said, "Because according to his wife, his experiments of late had taken a darker, less traditional route. She swears he had become fascinated with alchemy and was dabbling in different archaic formulas. And to that end, the intruder was holding a piece of paper in his hand as he ran off."

"Alchemy? How ludicrous," I replied as I poured. "No one in their right mind believes that nonsense. It is more superstition than science. I would have thought that a university professor would not stoop to such a medieval practice."

Holmes held out a quieting hand. "Do not be so judgmental, Watson. Many famous scientists dabbled in alchemy, most notably our countrymen Roger Bacon and Sir Isaac Newton."

My eyes widened in surprise. I had never heard such a thing and said as much. Holmes replied to my skepticism by saying, "I am not saying that any rational scientific mind would believe such a thing as making gold from baser elements, but I will, however, remind us all here that many inventions were discovered, albeit serendipitously, by the diligent practice of that dark science."

"Such as?" I asked.

Holmes replied as he counted them off on his long fingers, "Gunpowder, Prussian Blue, many of the poisons we know today, glass and ceramics, and for the fairer sex, cosmetics. These are but a few discoveries made by practicing alchemy. I can go on if you wish. The list is quite substantial."

Lestrade finally broke into the conversation as he wiped his nose, "So what you are saying is that maybe this man wasn't so much looking for how to turn lead into gold as he was possibly looking for the impetus to a new discovery or invention?"

"Quite right," said Holmes rather defeatedly. "It is possible and, indeed, probable that he was dabbling in alchemy only to ignite some more meaningful discovery that had been eluding him. I daresay many in the field are nothing more than frustrated inventors. It is a shame that modern chemistry has succumbed to the allure of the prostitute of commercialism."

Lestrade then replied cryptically, "Well then, I think it all the more prudent that you see his laboratory. There is something you need to see."

"And what about this intruder who rushed from the flat?" I asked.

Lestrade shrugged. "As it so happened, a beat constable, Parker is his name, was just up the street when he heard the shot. He saw the blackguard running from the place, gave chase, but there was too much ground to make up, and he was lost in the rain. We did a house to house to see if anyone saw anything. With but one exception, no one seemed to have paid any mind to the gunshot. It was only when they heard the scream did they choose to be nosey and look through their windows, but by then the murderer had absconded. In the meantime, Mrs. Austin, as mentioned, relayed that some of his students had been up in his little laboratory over the previous weeks so we are also ascertaining who they were, where they are, and rounding them up for questioning."

Lestrade rose and redonned his waterproof. "So, are you too engrossed in your own affairs to brave the elements and come give me your take on things?"

Sherlock gave me a look. "What say you, Watson? Are you willing to embrace a choleric Mother Nature, or do you prefer the comfortable boredom of Mrs. Hudson and the Times?"

Of the two evils, I made my decision. "I'll get my jacket and wellies."

After relaying our plans to Mrs. Hudson, we were off.

. . . .

The fifteen-minute jaunt down Baker Street was a quiet one, only momentarily coming to life when Lestrade coughed or sneezed or blew his nose. Holmes sat in quiet introspection, head bowed, resting his chin on his breast. Lestrade, like myself, had known Holmes for many years and knew he was not to be bothered with idle chat while in this contemplative state. I can only speculate that Holmes was turning in that great head of his how such an ancient and dead practice could lead to a person's untimely death in this modern age of scientific advancement. Intermittently, Lestrade and I would exchange glances in that silence then resettle our eyes out the window, watching the sheeting rain maul at the landscape of the Great City.

The professor's flat was only a short walk from the college, at the corner of Paget and Rawstorne Streets, with the entrance on Paget. The weather was kind enough to have slowed to an occasional drizzle, however, the wild wind still stung at any exposed skin.

The three of us alighted the taxi.

Taking in the surroundings, Holmes surveyed the area with a keen eye.

Pointing to a partially opened door with a sturdy constable sentried at its side, Lestrade said, "Our dead alchemist is up these stairs."

Surprisingly, Holmes replied, "I think I shall nibble on the morsels out here before sitting down to the meal within."

"Suit yourself. You won't mind if I wait inside for you then? No need for this cold to turn into pneumonia."

"Which way did the intruder run?"

Pointing, Lestrade said, "According to Parker, he first saw him on the opposite-side corner of Rawstorne and Paget, over there, while he was walking down Rawstorne from the opposite direction. He then gave chase. The man must have been young and fit to outrun Parker; he seems a sturdy and vigorous fellow, himself."

"Indeed," Holmes replied, and the manner and tone was such that I did not believe for a moment that he was agreeing with the inspector in his assessment of either the vigor of the constable or the sex of the intruder. Sherlock Holmes would agree with another's assessment only when he came to that same conclusion himself and not a moment before.

The inspector went inside the Austins' flat to wait for us while I followed Holmes up to the intersection of the two streets. Here, Paget ended at Rawstorne, so the murderer only had two options in his escape –left or right. Holmes looked left, up Rawstorne, I assume taking in the environs in which the constable came onto the scene, then right, down the opposite way the scoundrel made his escape. I noticed his acute eyes paying particular attention to the streetlamps, which lit the corners of the streets but did not reach the spaces between them. He then looked up at the buildings surrounding us. What he was looking for was anyone's guess. I would have thought more could be gleaned from the crime scene inside the flat, but Holmes knew this foul business better than anyone, and I am not one to needlessly question the sometimes circuitous routes he took in the ministrations of his detective work.

After having satisfied himself with the arrangement outside, Holmes finally turned, and we made our way back; but I noticed in our walk that he kept looking up at the building across from the Austins' flat. He then said to me. "We seem to have an audience. There is someone in the first floor flat across the street from the Austins who is watching from the shadows. His cigarette glow has given him away. He has been watching since our arrival. He looks to have the best view of the goings-on. Let us go and have a chat with him to find out what light he might shine on this affair."

We trudged through muddy puddles as we crossed the street, and Holmes rapped at the door with the tip of his umbrella. After a long moment and a second knock, the door jerked opened, and a balding gentleman stood before us holding a single lit candle. His only hair, red fading quickly to grey, was splayed out above his ears, and he had enormous and peculiarly round eyes, which looked upon us distastefully. His nose was arched and beaklike, giving him an avian—more precisely an owlish—appearance.

As Holmes was about to introduce us, the man cut him off by saying, "I talked to you lot already and told you what I saw, so be on your way."

He was about to close the door when my friend stuck a boot between the door and jamb. "But you have not spoken with *me*," replied Holmes coolly. It never ceased to amaze me that the man cared not whether his actions bordered on irritatingly intrusive. Indeed, I sometimes wondered if he received some grim pleasure doing things to purposely rattle those he wished to interrogate.

The man reopened the door slightly, glaring those saucer-sized eyes at my friend. "Then get my statement from the other bobbies," he huffed.

Smiling apologetically, Holmes replied, "I would much rather get my information first-hand, as I will more than likely be asking different questions than those previously posed to you."

The man sighed. "You're not going away then?"

Holmes only returned a blank stare.

"Fine. What do you want to know that I haven't already said?"

"First, may I ask what it is about our inquiry that has you so piqued?"

"You mean besides the fact that it's half-ten, and I've had about all I can stand of this weather?" The man nodded brusquely for us to come in. "It's freezing out and my situation isn't sufficient to heat the whole of London so come in so I can close the door."

It seemed to me that this gentleman showed the same annoyed behavior as Lestrade, as indeed we all seemed to be showing. The British constitution is notorious for its stiff upper lip, but in this prolonged twilight of winter, that lip was beginning to tremble.

We obliged, and he moved back, letting us step across the threshold before closing the door. He had a bent, apologetic gate despite his flippant manner. With only candlelight dancing off his face, he looked much older than his forty or so years.

Once inside, the stench of cigarettes assaulted my olfactory senses. Smoke wafted in a haze around the candlelight. I could almost feel the smoke in the air. In the gloom, one might consider the place to be on fire if it weren't for the fact burning tobacco smells nothing like burning wood. Even Holmes's smoking habits were amateurish compared to this man.

I stifled a cough.

Holmes said, "Thank you, Mr...."

"Montrose," the man replied. "Victor Montrose."

"I am Sherlock Holmes, and this is my colleague, Dr. Watson."

A knowing look and a small crease that may or may not have been a smile transformed his face, however only slightly. "Ah, the famous detective and his chronicler." That thin slit then suddenly disappeared, and his eyes narrowed and looked upon me. "I've read some of your accounts, doctor. Don't care for them. I'm not a man taken to reading fiction passed on as fact."

Surprised by the accusation, I replied, "I can assure you, Mr. Montrose, that every account has been utterly factual. I may have expounded on the inconsequentials, elaborated on the settings to make the stories more palatable to readers, but the facts of the story always remained intact. I have taken great pains in that endeavor."

"The skeletons of your stories may have been truth, but you indulged so much in putting meat on the bones of them that many died of obesity."

Holmes laughed, "Ah, a man after my own heart!"

Be it the weather or my old wound, but the man's irritation was growing on me, and Holmes was not helping the situation. A bit affronted, I replied, "Yes, well, we can stand here all night critiquing my writing abilities, or we can have a discussion about what has brought us to your door. Which would you rather?"

"Quite right, Watson, quite right. My apologies. Mr. Montrose, can you tell me what you saw and heard of the events earlier this evening?"

The man sighed again, which seemed to be his normal mode of respiring. "I was lying in my bed reading, which I do often, especially in this protracted agitated state of weather."

Holmes looked beyond the man at the vast, empty darkness. "And your wife?"

Montrose huffed at the statement. "I am not married."

That did not surprise me in the least, but I kept the thought to myself.

"And you have a room with a window that overlooks Paget Street?"

"Yes, that's right, my bedroom."

"May I be so bold as to ask permission to see it?"

"What the devil for?"

"It will help me in piecing together the events."

Montrose's high forehead beaded in thought for a moment. Finally, he said, "I suppose it would be alright. It's not made up for a dinner party, so mind the untidy nature of it."

He turned and waved us to follow him, but before he showed us up the steps to his first floor rooms, he turned to me and said, "This better not make it into any of the fantabulations you write."

"I wouldn't dream of it," I replied…

It was a room inundated in dirty linens and discarded garments crumpled in knee-high patches across the floor.

Unwashed plates and cutlery were stacked upon each other helter-skelter wherever there could be found a flat surface to hold them. Several large stacks of books, nonfiction I presumed, based on Montrose's loathing of its alter-ego, hid amongst the shadows given off in the candlelight. The ashtray next to the bed was filled to overflowing with ash and smoked cigarettes. The room reeked of sweat, urine and stale smoke. A basin partially filled with, I daresay what, lay at the foot of the bed, which was centered along the left wall. It was obvious that the man's entire home and habits had been reduced to this one room; it was both appalling and dismaying that a person could devolve to such a state as this.

Holmes crept through the malodourous debris, following Mr. Montrose, with me at the back. A window was centered on the wall in front of us. It was to this that Montrose led us as he took a moment to light another candle on his stand, apparently happy in the flickering gloom instead of showing off his slovenly habits with electric light.

Holmes looked out the window studying the layout of the street below and the building opposite. "How long have the Austins lived across from you?"

"About four years, I should think. I've been here ten myself."

"How well do you know them? asked Holmes.

Montrose treated me to a caustic stare, I presume only because Holmes's back was to the man. "By that, if you're asking in a roundabout way whether there was trouble in the marriage, only the wearer knows where the shoe pinches."

"No discourse that you are aware of then?"

"Now, don't go putting words in my mouth, I didn't say that. They've had their rows like anyone else. A few times I've seen a constable stopping over, probably summoned by a neighbor tired of the shouting. It's all noises of the jungle to me."

"So, their quarrels were such to attract the attention of neighbors," Holmes said more than asked.

Montrose lit another cigarette and replied dismissively, "Again, no more or less than some of the other rows that have taken place on the street. This isn't exactly Chelsea."

"Do you happen to know the nature of any of those arguments?" Holmes asked as his head maneuvered left and right, taking in the scene from this higher vantage point.

"None of my business and nor do I care."

As Holmes turned around and regarded the man directly for the first time since we entered the room, Montrose looked to one than the other of us and said, "You're barking up the wrong tree, Mr. Holmes, that much I can tell you. Whenever I have seen them about, they seemed fine. Whatever the nature of their quarrels it never seemed to affect them; they looked completely contented with each other—well, as content as a man and woman can be. For all we know, those contretemps could have been due to her making him a supper he didn't care for. Or just a bad day at work. I can assure you that Mr. Austin wasn't killed over a row with the missus. If that's what you're driving at then let me take over your detecting business. I could do better than that, and I could use the money."

Holmes gave out a hearty, if not sarcastic, laugh. Montrose didn't seem offended, which relayed to me his abilities in detection were sorely lacking.

"And how do you make your way if life, Mr. Montrose?"

"Excuse me?"

"What do you do for a living?" Holmes replied, hiding—but not completely—his exasperation.

The man hesitated then replied with no slight irritation. "You are indeed asking different questions than those posed by the bobbies."

"Did I not say so?" Holmes asked, surprised. "I am well aware of the inadequacies of professional law enforcement, which is why I wanted to speak to you in person."

"Yet, I fail to see—"

"I am quite certain you do, Mr. Montrose, but I do not. For whom do you work?"

"I work at City of London University, a lecturer."

"For how long and in what field?"

The man put out his half-smoked cigarette testily and said, "Say, what has any of this to do with a murder across the street?"

"Nothing, perhaps, but I am in the business of asking questions, and those questions, however inconvenient or seemingly inconsequential, have solved one or two little affairs over the years. So, I ask again, how long have you worked at the *same* university as the dead professor and in what field do you teach?"

When the question was put more succinctly, it was obvious the man then understood why Holmes asked it. A bit more subdued, he finally replied, "Ten years. And I am a lecturer in mathematics. But on this block alone you won't find less than three other men who call the university home."

"Thank you. Do you or have you interacted with Professor Austin in any capacity before?"

Montrose pulled out another cigarette from the holder he withdrew from his pocket, lit it, and replied in a puff of smoke, "Before two months ago I only ever saw the man in passing, walking down the halls of the university between classes. We never talked. I am not on his level"—this he said with an air of sarcasm. "Then, out of the blue, he approached me, knowing I work in mathematics, and asked me to work out some problems for him. He said it was for some speculative chemistry he was working on, which is more than likely why he did not take his aspirations to Professor Gruber, the Mathematics Chair. He did not wish to be laughed out of the room."

"Ah, these equations pertained to the alchemy experiments in his laboratory?"

Montrose gave a knowing look, "You have been told already about that, then?"

"Vaguely," Holmes returned.

"He gave me some base equations, but I could not get the answers he was looking for. After about three weeks of trying I gave up and told him the answers for which he was looking were impossible. He was certain I was wrong, that the math could indeed be worked out. He said he would test some greater minds, thanked me for my time, and that was that."

"He did not say who those greater minds were?"

"He did not, but I can tell you that none were Professor Gruber. I mentioned to him what Austin was up to, and his retort could be heard 'round the entire university. From there, the news made its way through the halls like a wildfire. He was harassed and became the butt of jokes, to be sure, but he had brought it on himself. Alchemy? Really! There was even talk of disciplinary measures. But as with all folly, it soon died down, and in the last few weeks things seemed to have rather gotten back to normal for him professionally."

"Thank you. Most helpful. So, then, now on to more immediate things. Tell me about this evening. Pray, leave nothing out."

Montrose shrugged. "A peaceful night by any measure. If there was anything nefarious going on before the murder it was drowned out by the rain and wind. I was lying in bed smoking and reading when I heard what sounded like a pistol shot. It was high-pitched, not bombastic like a rifle."

"Thank you for noticing that differentiation. Most helpful. Many would not have given the sound itself any thought."

This rare compliment from Holmes seemed to please the man, and he went on with a less belligerent tone. "I roused myself from my book, jumped from my bed and went to the window. The Austins' front door was open, which I could see from my window, despite this never-ending, bloody gale. Within moments of reaching the window, I saw the constable appear. He was running down Rawstorne as fast as the weather would let him. He was blowing his whistle and yelling out to stop. Just after that, I heard Mrs. Austin scream. The bobby must have heard it too, given up the chase, and returned to see if he could be of assistance…and here you are."

"You did not see the intruder yourself?" Holmes asked.

The sanguinity that Holmes was hoping to bring out in the man suddenly perished with the question. "As I said already," Montrose replied with heated impatience, "he was out the door by the time I got to the window. I don't move as quick as I did in my younger days. I only saw the constable giving chase."

"This was how long ago?" asked my friend, once again turning his attention out the window.

Montrose shrugged. "I don't know," he said with irritation, "an hour and a half."

"And the weather at the time?"

"Bloody awful! Where have you been the last few weeks?"

"By that, I mean was there a break in the rain when this event transpired?"

"No, there was not."

Holmes turned from the window and gave the room one more cursory look. "Thank you, Mr. Montrose. You have been most helpful."

"Like I said, this is all information I have *already* given."

"Not all of it."

"Everything *relevant*," he replied with a cynical sneer.

"I'll thank you for permitting me to be the judge of that."

"Yes, well your *thoroughness* has just wasted almost fifteen minutes of my time—time I cannot get back."

"Our apologies," Holmes replied with forced deference. "We shall show ourselves out. Thank you for your time."

Once outside, I said, "You know, Holmes, I am not a man readily given over to exasperation, but that Montrose fellow was singularly irritating. To think that I embellish my stories. You know that those stories are, despite some artistic flourishes here and there, completely factual."

Clapping his umbrella tip onto the cobblestone as we walked back across the avenue, Holmes replied, "It is not like you, Watson, to let such a drudge of a man get under your collar. We shall chalk it up to misplaced agitation due to your ailing shoulder. I know this weather has not been kind to it."

Rubbing it I replied, "Perhaps you are right. It has been most troublesome these last few weeks. And frankly, you have said much worse about my writing, so I'm not sure why this man's assessment bothered me."

As we made the opposite walkway, I then asked, "Were you able to glean anything pertinent from the information Montrose gave you?"

"Some. I will say that based on what I've been told so far, someone is lying."

"Do you think maybe the professor wasn't as gracious as described in his spurning of Montrose's failed attempt at those equations? Certainly, belittling a man in his position could have enraged Montrose enough to do this deed himself."

"If that were the case then who was our intrepid young constable chasing, a decoy, perhaps? That is entirely possible, perhaps probable. Yet, I need more data to put this little puzzle together."

As we stopped and Holmes bent to inspect the door and lock of the Austin home, he then said with a wry grin, "And regarding our new acquaintance's analysis of your writing prowess, do not despair, Watson. I would not lose sleep over any literary critique given by a man who reads romances in his spare time."

"Romances?"

"Yes, Watson, Romances. Most of the books were turned over or in too much shadow to discern, but the one on his bed was titled, Villette, a Bronte novel, if memory serves."

Lestrade was at the top of the stairs when we stepped through to the large, square entranceway. "Up here, gentlemen," he said with a wave.

Holmes examined the carpeted steps as we ascended. "The floor is quite wet, indeed. Did anyone check for dampness on the carpeting when they entered?"

"Unfortunately, not," replied Lestrade. "When Parker gave up the chase and went back to see where the screams were coming from, he saw the open door and dashed up the stairs, thinking there was still another intruder. That is at least partially his wet trail you see."

"Well, that's unfortunate," said Holmes.

"Unfortunate for you, perhaps, but Parker did the right thing, thinking someone's life was still in danger. We can't worry about muddying up a crime scene if there are lives to be saved."

"Quite right," Holmes replied. "Still…"

"Do you wish to talk to the widow or see the crime scene first?" the inspector asked as we made the landing.

"The crime scene, of course," said Holmes.

"Just to get your bearings," Lestrade then said pointing around them, "that room under the stairs to the loft is the Austins' bedroom. That is where Mrs. Austin was when she heard the shot. The kitchen is through there with the dining room beyond in a large alcove that opens onto back stairs. The parlor is through that door. There is a second sitting room through that archway. That is where the widow is currently at rest with Parker, there, at the entrance to attend to whatever she may need while we investigate."

Holmes and I both gave the young constable a once-over. He had removed his waterproof, which lay in a pile on the floor next to him. His thick, brown hair clung to his forehead as it dried out from the inclement weather, and his uniform, though mostly dry, was discoloured from wetness about his collar, cuffs, and pantlegs. He was a vigorous looking man with a chiseled, clean-shaven jaw that bulged a bit on one side, thin lips, and intense blue eyes. His musculature filled out his uniform impressively, and I could see why Lestrade would think it would take some feat to outrun someone with such an athletic build. Yet a head start and weather that would obscure anything over a half-block away surely tipped the balance in favor of the blackguard in his escape. His demeanor, as he silently looked upon us as we walked by, was one of disappointment. He no doubt also felt as though the murderer should not have escaped his clutches.

The stairway to the loft was open with a sturdy banister on one side and a high wall to accommodate the ample ceiling height on the other. At the top of the steps was an open door, and here Lestrade held out his hand and bid us enter the room.

The area before us was a spectacular display of test tubes, Bunsen burners, placards of the periodic table of elements, glass and rubber tubing and receptacles of all shapes and sizes, all lit by electric light. The whole place had a haphazard, wild look about it—a jungle of laboratory paraphernalia. Along the wall to the left was a bookshelf filled with works from Watt, Faraday, Newton, Frankland, and Strindberg (who I knew not as a scientist but as a playwright and novelist), as well as some names that were unfamiliar to me. Next to it was a glass cabinet filled with numerous chemicals. I am sure that if Holmes had devoted his life to chemistry instead of the art of detecting, this would have been a good start to his laboratory.

Our murdered alchemist, Mr. Austin, lay slumped over the desk to our right. There was a small, blood-soaked hole in his white shirt in the area just below his right shoulder blade. The coppery scent of blood was faint yet discernable. In warmer weather, certainly up in a loft, it would be overpowering by now, but the cold climate had kept the odour at bay. The desk itself was centered at the only window in the loft.

Holmes glanced at the floor then took in the state of the room before us before we gathered around the dead man and his desk. He then briefly peered out the window past our reflections at a dark, washed-out courtyard centered amongst the buildings. "No one would have been able to see anything from this height and at such a distance between habitations, especially in this weather, which blurs everything." Holmes then asked as brought his critical eye closer to home, "What do you make of the wound, Watson?"

As I examined the body, I couldn't help but notice that the professor was young and comely, with dark hair and square, set features, not the rounded, balding and bespectacled type usually given over to academia, which Victor Montrose fit perfectly. A cup of cold tea was set before him, and he was still grasping his pencil when the fatal shot found its mark. I set about to examine the entrance wound a few inches below his right shoulder blade. I then pulled the body up from the desk to examine the larger exit wound slightly lower in the front. "It almost certainly went through his liver. This was not a survivable wound. It looks like the bullet is lodged in the front drawer of his desk."

"Yes, we'll be retrieving that shortly," remarked Lestrade. "Do you think death was instantaneous?"

"No," I replied. "I see no evidence of spurting, so I do not think the hepatic artery was hit. The exit wound is of sufficient size that if the artery was indeed hit the blood would have spurted out with every heartbeat. Nothing I see suggests that. On the contrary, the blood seems to have pooled in his lap. That would tell me that he more than likely exsanguinated—bled to death. It would have been a few minutes at most before he succumbed to his wound, but he would have been rendered unconscious from blood loss sometime before that."

"And these are the papers on which the professor was working when he was murdered?" Holmes asked, referring to a stack of about a dozen papers in front of the dead professor on the desk.

"Yes, that's right," replied Lestrade stifling a cough and wiping his nose. "I looked them over myself. They are chemical equations of one sort or another. Between these and the paper the murderer ran off with, that is why I decided on asking for your assistance."

Holmes picked up the papers from the desk and looked over the first few pages. After about the fourth page he folded them up but kept them. He *hmphed*. "Mostly synthesis reactions and double displacement reactions. Common chemistry. Nothing of the speculative chemistry Montrose spoke of."

Lestrade knitted his brow. "Speculative chemistry? Where did you hear that from? Who is Montrose?"

"The neighbor across the street, Mr. Montrose."

"Ah, the smoker."

"Did you know the *smoker* was a professor at the same university as Austin, albeit in a more junior capacity?"

"I did not," replied Lestrade.

"Did you not think to ask during your normal line of questioning?"

"I can see no relevance in a neighbor's situation when asking if he had seen the perpetrator of murder running from a murder scene," he said with a bit of annoyance.

"Honestly, Lestrade, your lack of imagination in methods of inquiry are uninspiring."

The inspector pulled out his handkerchief and wiped his now ruddy nose. "Have I learned nothing from you Holmes, after all these years? I at least had the sense to know when I was out of my element to bring in someone with more expertise." He then gave Holmes a wry smile. "Anyway, you only found that out because *I* asked you here. You could just as easily be back at Baker Street playing that whining violin of yours and missing out on all this."

Holmes began looking more closely at the desk. "Touché, Lestrade, how prescient of you." He opened the top drawer. I saw nothing in it. However, I could tell by the look on Holmes's face that its emptiness spoke volumes to him. Yet he said nothing, closed the drawer, turned, and began looking over the laboratory equipment.

Lestrade's eyes then became wide with excitement. "Oh, yes, I almost forgot. You might find this interesting. Maybe more interesting than the dead professor." He motioned for Holmes to follow him down to the end of a long counter at the opposite end of the room as the body. It seemed that all the vine-like coils and tubing seemed to be meandering their way to this particular area. It was here that we could see the fruits of Professor Austin's labour. One long stretch of copper tubing ended at the opening of a small, glass flask. Dripping from the mouth of this small copper tube was a golden liquid which, it seemed to me, congealed or coalesced into a small, irregularly shaped fragment at the bottom of the flask as it rested in tiny amount of clear, yellowish liquid.

As Holmes inspected the detritus in the flagon, I ran my eyes along the tubing, following it back to its origination at the opposite end hidden amongst piles of books and large flasks and graduated cylinders in need of washing. Here, sitting on a mesh-metal screen was a small, book-sized block of what to my eyes looked like lead. Another bluish liquid was awash and bubbling over the metal like an acid and was being collected through the mesh into a funnel. From there, the journey wound its way through several boiling liquids and condensers, which made its way back down the counter to where Holmes and Lestrade were standing.

"Holmes, there is what looks to be a small block of lead at this end being dissolved by some unknown substance, possibly an acid of some sort," said I.

Holmes ran down to where I now stood, inspected the block, then followed the setup with his trained eye from one end, through all its twists and turns and tubes, all the way back to the small piece of gold material in the flask at the end.

As Holmes inspected all this, Lestrade said, "Now, to my untrained eye it looks as though Professor Austin just might have solved the mystery of turning lead into gold."

"Or that is what he wanted everyone to believe," replied my friend.

"Looks like gold to me."

"It could be pyrite, 'fool's gold'," said Holmes. He examined it further. "However, pyrite has a more cuboidal appearance to it. This might actually be gold."

"Could it be that he really discovered the ultimate secret of alchemy?" I asked. "The ramifications of this discovery have worldwide significance. A country would pay a king's ransom to know this secret."

"Indeed," remarked Lestrade. "Murder would be a small price to pay for such a discovery."

"It is an impossibility," retorted Holmes steadfastly. "You were not an hour ago lamenting on that very remark."

"Yet, how do you explain this?" asked Lestrade.

"Ah, if only answers came just when you summon them. If that were the case, I could have saved myself a fight to the death at Reichenbach and three years of my life, not to mention countless other inconveniences throughout my career.

My methods do not work that way, you know that, Lestrade. Rest assured; the answers will come. They always do."

Holmes then decided to inspect the bookshelf and rummaged through the titles. He, at last, came upon a small volume bound in cracked leather, written in French. Holmes read the title out loud, "Wonders of the Alchemy of Compte De Saint Germain."

"Who the devil is he?" asked Lestrade.

"He was one of the most enigmatic figures in history," said Holmes. "No one knows with certainty who he was or from where he came, but he was a most intimate friend to many of the royalty of Europe a century and a half ago. He was believed by some to be five-hundred years old. It is because of this that he is also well-renowned as one of the most powerful alchemists who ever lived."

"Is it then possible that this volume is where Austin found the solution to alchemy?" I asked.

Holmes waved the statement off. "I have read it myself, Watson. A dry, fantastical piece of fiction that would no doubt elicit full assault of conscience from our friend across the street. No, if the elixir of life and other nonsense were indeed written between the pages of this tome, someone long before our dead professor would have stumbled upon it."

"Well, he stumbled upon something," said I. "Maybe the more relevant work is on the paper that was stolen."

Lestrade asked, "So, having now seen all this, what do you make of it all, so far?"

"It poses several interesting theories, none of which I am as yet ready to propound. There are still missing threads that I need to knit together this little mystery. I believe I need to now speak with the widow."

It was then that Jefferies, Lestrade's right-hand man, popped his gigantic head in the doorway and said, "We were able to find a few of Austin's students at a pub, King George's Seat, just down from the university."

"And?" Lestrade asked impatiently.

"And none are suspects. The publican insists they were all there since at least eight, an hour before the murder."

"Do any have an idea who our mysterious intruder could have been?"

"No, sir."

"Bloody hell!" Lestrade exclaimed. "I was sure with one of those students we'd have our man."

"One bloke I spoke to, a—" here he consulted his note pad "—Geoffrey Carmichael did say, however, that only a handful of students were permitted into the laboratory at his flat—those who were helping him with these *experiments*. And of those students, there was one who was not present at the pub: Archibald Merriweather. But none pegged him as the type who would shoot a man in cold blood. Very bookish and a bit of a dandy. Probably never held a pistol in his life—their words, not mine."

"Well, perceptions can be wrong, Jefferies. I think we have our number one suspect."

"You have *a* suspect, not necessarily *the* suspect," reminded Holmes. "You cast your net and pull out a fish, and there you have your Moby Dick, not even considering whether your catch is a white whale or a run-of-the-mill herring. You need to cast a wider net."

"Do you not at least think it odd that one other person with access to the laboratory was not with his fellow students, while an unknown person murders the professor and slinks off into the night with what might be a formula that will change the world?"

"You deal with conjecture, Lestrade. You seem comfortable there. I shall hang my hat on fact."

Then, it seemed, Holmes began to lose interest quickly in this back and forth and began to look over the professor's papers, once again until we could excuse ourselves to talk to the widow.

I, on the other hand, offered a question of my own to Jefferies. "Did they mention if they were close to any breakthroughs?"

"It seems the professor was very secretive about his formulas. They knew certain ingredients but had no idea of what quantities and in what order. They were only there to, and I quote, 'Fetch me this, get me that, turn that on, turn this off when I say.' That sort of thing."

I then asked, "In our conversation with the gentleman across the street, he mentioned that he was asked but could not produce answers to some elaborate equations posed to him by Mr. Austin. When he could not furnish the desired result, Austin said he would press upon greater minds to come up with the answer."

Jefferies was giving me a telling nod as I spoke and offered, "I didn't know about that, doctor, but I did ask if they knew of anyone outside the circle of students who might have known about what Austin was doing or who might have been assisting in his work. They said the entire university knew of it thanks to a bit of gossip, but as far as they knew no one outside of them helped in the experiments."

"That increases our circle of inquiry considerably," Lestrade lamented. "It may be that our golden thread lies with that *greater mind* that Montrose was alluding to, but now our suspect pool has grown to the size of an entire university. How's that for casting a wider net, Holmes?" With that, he pulled out his handkerchief, sneezed, and blew his nose, once again.

It was here that we were all startled by a burst of laughter from Sherlock Holmes.

"And what do you find so funny, Holmes?" asked the inspector. "Is it my blasted cold or the prospect of having to interrogate an entire academic institution?"

"Neither," remarked Holmes. "I must apologize to you, Lestrade; and Watson, I believe we will have to make a similar act of contrition to our newest acquaintance, Mr. Montrose. We have indeed wasted everyone's time in this matter."

"What on earth are you talking about, Holmes?"

"First, I must lay at least some blame with you, Lestrade."

"Me? What did I do?"

Holding up the papers in which he'd been holding and now obviously scrutinizing with a more studious eye, he said, "Did you not tell me that you looked over these papers yourself?"

"You know I did. It was because of those papers that I sought your assistance."

"And they were in the exact order in which you found them?"

"They were."

Holmes gave Lestrade a critical stare, at which Lestrade gave a face as one who was going over in his head the steps he had taken earlier. Then, his face fell. "You are quite right, Holmes. When I was looking over the papers, I believe I laid them to the side face-up as I went from paper to paper instead of face-down."

"Exactly," replied Holmes. "So, the first paper becomes the last and the last first."

"Why would it matter? You said yourself that there was nothing of import on them."

"I had only looked through the first few pages. While you felt the need to increase your work by pining over the possible list of suspects from an entire university, I lessened it to but one by reading the rest of these papers. But if the papers were in the correct order, I could have deduced this earlier."

Lestrade's face began to turn the same colour as his nose. "I read over those papers, and I saw nothing that would be of any help in catching a murderer."

Holmes smiled. "You did one thing right, inspector—you called upon me."

At this, he produced a sheet of paper from the ones in his hand and gave it to Lestrade, who gave it a cursory glance and said, "So what is so special about this paper? I see no help in our investigation anywhere on here."

Holmes replied, "It looks like a list of elements, yes?"

Lestrade handed me the paper. On it were listed some random elements. After I glanced at it, I also remarked, "I have to agree with Lestrade. Unless you enlighten us, I see nothing of import here. It is just a random list of elements." Then something struck me, and I asked, "Do you suppose this might be the list of ingredients needed to turn lead into gold? Is it possible our murderer already knew the *what* of the experiment so did not need to abscond with this list and only needed to make off with the *how* that was written on that paper?"

I could tell by his demeanor that Holmes was disappointed with our inability to recognize what he could so clearly see. Yet, more often than not, this was the usual state of affairs. "Your theory is flawed, Watson, as we shall see momentarily. I shall first want to draw your attention on how I recognized the *who*. First, notice how the last *n* in Nitrogen trails off. That was the last word he wrote before he died. That is how I knew this was the top sheet of paper."

"That could be anything," Lestrade argued half-heartedly. "Being interrupted or startled while writing that list could have caused the same mark." He knew Holmes was correct disproportionately more than he was wrong, yet Lestrade, even after all these years, would not let go of a missed clue on his behalf. It always amused me, but the inspector's pigheadedness, often a detriment in cases such as this, was also the reason why Holmes always called upon him in times of trouble.

"You would be correct," Holmes went on, "and this de minimis may have escaped my eye if it weren't for the fact that the professor died with a pencil still in his hand."

I asked, "How could he have known his murderer? His back was turned away from the door. The wound plays that out."

Holmes casually walked over to the desk. It was then that I understood. I could see distinctly his reflection in the window beyond the desk smiling at me. "You see, Watson, the window and the light from the room make for a wonderful mirror. Professor Austin could see fairly clearly who it was that fired the fatal shot."

"So, let's cut to the chase," Lestrade said. "Who killed the professor?"

Holmes turned from the window. "I need to put things right in my own mind before I reveal the blackguard. Patience, Lestrade. You will have your murderer soon enough. I think it now time to go down and have a chat with the widow to see what light she can shine on the events of this dreadful night. If the conversation goes as I think it shall, Mrs. Austin will give us our murderer shortly."

He then called over Jefferies and said something to him in hushed tones that, at the time, I could not discern.

Then, we all proceeded down the stairs of the loft. Jefferies continued down the entrance stairs while we went to the sitting room. When he saw us, Constable Parker, who had been leaning against the wall, scratching at his jaw, resumed his dutiful, at-attention stance. He had the guilty look as one who was caught slacking in his duties, although I doubt anyone would have remonstrated him since he had been at the scene since the beginning. Lestrade attempted dismissing him, but Holmes spoke up, "No, please do us the favor, constable, of staying nearby. You have been here from the first, and the widow might feel more at ease knowing you were close at hand. We may also have some questions of you before this matter can be cleared up entirely and we make an arrest."

His chiseled face wrinkled, and he bore what appeared to be an uncomfortable look. "An arrest? You found the murderer, then?"

"We have," replied Holmes casually.

The young constable was taken aback. Masculine pride is a fickle thing, especially for someone with virility in abundance. His immediate chase of the man yielded no results, and we had been there for only a short time and already had our man, if only in theory and not yet in actuality. His demeanor articulated an obvious aversion to being shown up.

With that, Holmes, Lestrade, and I went into the sitting room.

The widow, swathed in a plush dressing gown, made more for warmth than appeal, dabbed at her swollen eyes. She was a beautiful young woman, even in this state. Her flaxen locks curled in long waves around a porcelain face. Her blue eyes, glassy with tears, looked bluer in that mournful state, and her dainty freckles could just be discerned due to the flush of her wet cheeks. In her delicate fingers, she held a well-used handkerchief.

"Mrs. Austin, this is Sherlock Holmes and Dr. Watson. I often call them in on unusual cases. They have been a huge help to Scotland Yard over the years. I hope you don't mind."

She shook her head, no, and said in a soft Irish accent, "Your reputation precedes you, Mr. Holmes. I am very thankful for any assistance you might offer." To Lestrade, she then asked, "Did I hear correctly that you have found the murderer of my husband?"

Lestrade spoke up, "Yes, Mrs. Austin. Yes, we did." He then cleared his throat and shot Holmes that uncomfortable look he always wore when he wasn't privy to all Holmes's facts.

My friend then took the lead. "It seemed from the very beginning we were missing some of the facts of this most unusual case. I am hoping you might be able to clear up some of that fog, Mrs. Austin. That would go a long way in proving our suspect. Please tell me everything as you remember it. I apologize for taxing you unduly like this, but it is very important."

She looked each of us over with sullen eyes then nodded her agreement. "I went to bed a bit early. The weather of late has made for melancholy and I knit to pass the time while my husband works in his laboratory up in the loft."

"Does he spend much time up there?"

"It is his life, Mr. Holmes. He is married to chemistry, and I am but his mistress. I once shared that same singular obsession for it but gave it up to be a wife and someday a mother."

"So, you are familiar with the workings of chemistry?"

"Yes, of course. That is how we met. I was once his student."

"Yes, well, please, continue with this evening."

"It was a little past nine when I heard what I thought an explosion. I know the time because the clock had just chimed no more than a minute or two before then. I turned the corner to run up the stairs to make sure Harry was alright when someone in a dark mackintosh came running down the stairs with a paper in one hand and a pistol in the other. He knocked me over and ran down the stairs out into the night. After I regained myself, I went up to check on my husband, and he was dead. I screamed, and a moment or two later the constable arrived. He calmed me down, led me to the sitting room, and here I've been ever since."

"Was it raining at the time of the incident?"

"Yes, it had been raining nonstop since midday."

"Do you know where he keeps his papers?"

She shrugged. "On his desk, I should think."

"He would not have left any out on a counter somewhere, say within reach of the door to the loft?"

She looked perplexed. "I don't quite understand."

"Well, the floor going up the entrance stairs and even to the doorway of the loft was wet, yet the floor in the laboratory itself was dry."

At this revelation, I thought back. It had never entered my mind the state of the floor in the loft while marveling at the surroundings and the dead man.

"It is entirely possible he would leave a paper lying about absentmindedly. He had been running himself rather thin of late. Late nights in the laboratory, classes the next day and all that."

"Understood. Entirely possible," my friend replied with an incredulous conviction in his tone. "Yet, if that missing paper had on it some grand, world-changing experiment the results of which can be readily seen in your husband's laboratory—the changing of lead into gold, which seems to be the consensus of my colleagues—I doubt very much that he would have just let it sit about the countertops ripe for ruination from a spilled concoction or Bunsen burner flame. I deduce that he would have taken great pains to keep it secret and out of harm's way."

She nodded ascent. "As I stated, any important papers he usually has on his desk or in one of its drawers. But I cannot divulge what was on the paper taken for I was not privy to the practicalities of his experiments. Possibly, that paper is not important at all."

"And you may be onto something, Mrs. Austin," said Holmes as he shot Lestrade and myself a smug glance. "

"Then there is the time it took for the intruder to leave," he went on."

She gave Holmes another doe-eyed stare. "I am still in the dark as to what you are getting at, Mr. Holmes."

"I surmise a time of approximately thirty seconds to more likely a minute for the murderer to shoot your husband, find that paper—without somehow soiling the floor—and bound down two flights of stairs out into the night."

"Yes, that sounds about right. I am sure it was less than a minute."

"Yet, Mr. Montrose across the street was lying in bed reading when he heard the shot. His bed is but ten feet from his window. When he heard the shot, he—as he said himself attests— immediately got up from his bed and went to his window. Allowing a second or two to register the sound then getting up from his bed I propose ten, fifteen seconds at most. At best, that would be about the time the intruder was running down the loft stairs where you encountered him. Yet, when he looked out into the night, he was sure your door was already open, and Constable Parker was giving chase. You see, Mrs.

Austin, the time frame doesn't add up. However, I will allow that the mind is not trained to remember things precisely in adverse conditions. It is entirely possibly, even probable, that Mr. Montrose took longer to get to the window than he remembered. I also believe the culprit was known by the professor. What brigand would be out on a night like this and just happen upon an unlocked door? Possibly, the two exchanged words in the doorway, and he forcibly took the paper from your husband. Knowing he was outmatched physically; your husband went back to retrieve the pistol he keeps in his desk drawer. There was a struggle, and that is when he was shot, and thus began this whole affair."

"Yes, that must be it," Mrs. Austin replied exasperated. "Like I said, I pay no mind to the comings and goings. It happened so frequently of late."

Lestrade spoke up, brow knitted in confusion, "I saw no pistol in his desk drawer."

"That is because it was not there," replied Holmes. "However, there was a faint outline in the dust of the drawer where a pistol had been. Lofts can be notoriously dusty spaces. And with the light at my back, I could see a faint outline of a pistol—a Webley, if I know my firearms."

I then retorted, "That could not be how the events unfolded. He was sitting at his desk with his back turned when he was shot."

"Ah, Watson, that brings us finally to the *who* that I began to explain in the loft. Mrs. Austin, please tell me what sparked your murderous plan? Was it the affair you are having with Constable Parker?"

Her countenance washed in successive waves of fear, panic, and anger. "What on earth would make you think it was I who killed my husband?"

"Precisely, Fiona—may I call you by your given name?—because your husband told me?"

The woman was flabbergasted, and I must say, both Lestrade and myself held similar countenances at the remark."

"That is outrageous! How could he tell you anything? He is dead."

"Quite right, but your shot was not an instant kill. He lingered just enough to write your name on this." He showed her the paper.

"Why it is nothing but a list of elements—fluorine, iodine, oxygen, sodium, gold, sulfur, titanium, nitrogen. I am still in the dark."

"Tsk, tsk, Mrs. Austin. I should have thought it immediately clear to you how your husband penned his killer. That list is the name of his murderer. As you well know, the Periodic Table of Elements lists all known elements and among other things, abbreviates them into one or two letters. This list of elements can be rewritten using their abbreviations. F for fluorine, I for iodine, O for oxygen, and NA for sodium. Put them together and you have Fiona. Gold is Au, Sulfur is S Titanium is Ti, and Nitrogen is N. Austin. Fiona Austin. There you have it. Your husband hid your name in the table of elements so you could not see later that he had fingered you and dispose of the evidence of your culpability before authorities arrived. But you could not pull this off yourself. You needed help and found it in your lover, Parker."

Lestrade went to the archway where Parker had been on guard, but he was no longer there. "Bloody hell! Parker has got away. He must have overheard us." He ran to the top of the stairs and yelled down to the constable at the entrance, "Find Constable Parker! He has been implicated in the murder of Professor Austin."

It was then that he heard a scuffle in the back of the flat. He and I ran to the kitchen while Holmes stayed with Mrs. Austin. It was here that we found Constable Parker on the floor with Jefferies' mammoth bulk on top of him. Yet even with his considerable size, he needed the help of another constable to subdue the man.

"Mr. Holmes was right," Jefferies said to me. "When the game was up, he tried to make his way out the back door, and we were there waiting for him."

It was here that Holmes with Mrs. Austin in tow came into the room. Her eyes filled with tears once more when she saw her man helpless on the floor. "Please let him go. It was I who killed my husband. It was all of my doing."

"Don't do this, Fiona," Parker grunted. "There is no need for you to face the hangman. I killed him. He was a worthless, hopeless eccentric who spent all his time chasing fairy tales. I did it. I did it for her. How could anyone ignore a jewel such as Fiona? She wanted a family, and he wanted fool's gold. If he wanted to waste his own life, then I say let him have at it, but he was wasting hers as well. I could not stand it any longer."

"Only one pulled the trigger," said I. "Who should be believed?"

Holmes replied waving the paper, "I believe the dead husband."

"Both can share a rope at the gallows, for all I care," said Lestrade.

As Lestrade grabbed the woman by the arm, she cried out, "Damn you, Harry! Damn you for my ruination!"

Parker, after having been wrestled back to his feet and handcuffed, spat, "He didn't deserve to live. That monster even refused divorce. We had no other option but murder."

"There are always other options, sir," said my friend. "Murder just happens to be the easiest means to the end you desired."

Once the pair was removed, Lestrade said, "All we have to do is find the murder weapon, and this case will be wrapped up in a nice, neat bow."

"I am sure you will find it hidden somewhere within the house but not hidden very well," said Holmes. "There would have been no need since there was almost no evidence that pointed to her, and they had too small of a window in which to work. My guess would be under a loose floorboard or some such. It should not take much convincing now that they confessed for them to relay its whereabouts."

"So, what do you make of that setup in the loft?" I asked. "Did he really succeed in turning lead into gold?"

Holmes gave a quick chuckle, "Evidence is not always what it appears, Watson. Given enough clues, one can deduce much. For example, you were correct in your assessment of the lead bar. A weak acid was poured over it giving the appearance of dissolving the bar. The yellow solution dripping over the *gold* was picric acid, which I noticed among the chemicals in the professor's cabinet. She had to rearrange things quickly to get it set up just so to look like it was following some systematic flow from the lead to the gold, and she did it marvelously. She had obviously been planning this for some time, probably experimenting with different arrangements and chemicals while her husband was at university, and her knowledge in chemistry helped her to that end."

"And the gold in the flask?" I asked.

"Ah, yes, the *piece de resistance:* the gold in the flask was a gold filling from a tooth Constable Parker had removed. That was cunning, I must say. The swelling, though diminishing was still noticeable, and at least once I noticed the constable playing at his jaw tentatively. No doubt the extraction site is still sore. A quick look inside his mouth will bear this out."

As we all walked out of the kitchen together, Holmes added, "The plan was almost flawless. Had Mrs. Austin not been so hesitant in her aim and hit the heart she was no-doubt targeting, this might have had a better ending for them."

"How did you know they were having an affair?" I asked.

"Love always seems to have in its grasp those who perpetrate this kind of crime, Watson. That is why I stay clear of the sentiment. It has its uses but can very easily stray into darker realms."

"I've gotten used to your ways, Holmes," Lestrade said in a satisfied tone. "There was once a time where I would be fuming for missing what is so obvious to you. But I am interminably grateful that we are on the same side, and I count myself lucky to have the relationship we have where I can call upon you at all hours of the night for your help. In the end, catching the guilty is all that matters."

"Amen to that," said I. It was then that I felt a tickling at my nose then let loose with a resounding sneeze. In that immediate aftermath, I noticed for the first time that I felt a bit drained.

"Watson, you do not look well. We shall leave you to finish up here, Lestrade. Watson needs the comforts of Baker Street and a hot cup of honey tea. I think he has got your cold."

"Whatever you do," remarked the inspector, "steer clear of the porous plaster."

The End

The Problem at Witney

The summer morning was a warm and bright one. I had made up my mind, as I roused myself from my bed, to spend the day roaming Portman Square Garden, taking in the rare, beautiful London day. That is until I left my bedroom and saw Sherlock Holmes sitting at his desk with the window open, sipping tea and reading a telegram. When he looked upon me, a glint in his eager eyes, I knew straight away that he had other plans.

"Beautiful day, is it not, Watson?" he seemed to say with an air more of propriety than actuality.

I eyed my friend with some open suspicion as I went to the tray Mrs. Hudson had brought up and poured myself a cup of tea. "It is," I replied.

"Did you have any plans for the day?" he asked.

"None that cannot be broken," I replied, sipping my tea. Nodding to the telegram I asked, "Lestrade find something to pique your interest?"

"No, no," Holmes replied as he rose from the seat and handed me the telegram. "It seems the agreeable weather of late has tamed even the wild animals of London. This is from one Milton Hughes. He is the owner of a hotel in Witney, just west of Oxford."

He handed me the telegram and began relaying its contents as I tried to read along. I eventually put the telegram down and let him explain it to me, which seemed his real intention from the first. "It seems one of Mr. Hughes' lodgers, a Francis Erdley, has been found murdered in his room, and a necklace of quite some value, a gift for his sister whom he was on his way to see, has been stolen. The distraught hotel owner has asked for my help in the matter, as it would be a black mark on his business should this not come to a fruitful conclusion."

"I am sure the dead patron's family might also like to see a *fruitful conclusion* as well," I added dryly.

Holmes, as was his custom, was not listening to the remark but tapping his chin thoughtfully. "Does that name sound familiar to you, Watson—Hughes, Milton Hughes. Yes, I am sure I've heard it before."

"It does not ring any bells with me. Why don't you look it up in that index of yours?"

He waved his hand, "No time for that. I've consulted the Bradshaw, and we must depart now for Paddington if we are to make the next train. What say you, Watson? Up for some country air? If the weather is this comely in London, just imagine how it will be in the Cotswolds."

"I will admit, this sounds more interesting than the day at Portman Square I had initially envisioned." As I took my last sip of tea and grabbed my bowler, I asked, "Will I be needing my service revolver?"

"I should think not," he replied. "Ours will be a purely investigative pursuit and an intriguing one at that."

"How so?" I asked as we headed for the door. "A dead man in a hotel room and a stolen necklace of some value hardly seems to be the type of crime that you, of all people, would consider *intriguing*."

"Did you not read the telegram I gave you?" He did not give me time to answer. "It is intriguing precisely because this gentleman had guards outside his bedroom door and placed around the hotel, yet someone was still able to gain access to his room, kill him, and make off with a necklace with a sizeable ruby as its centerpiece."

"What kind of person feels the need to be guarded thusly?"

"That was a piece of the puzzle left out of the telegram and one that greatly fascinates me. Come, Watson, let us find out what is what in Witney."

. . . .

We were surprised to see a constabulary wagon waiting for us when our train pulled into Oxford. A tall, woolly-haired officer recognized us through our cabin window and motioned for us to disembark. He approached us, hand out in greeting. "Hullo, Mr. Holmes, Dr. Watson, I am Chief Constable Mear. I hope you don't mind being picked up here. It's quicker to get to Witney by road than rail from Oxford. There's always a dreadful wait in Yarnton before the train goes on to Witney. I can apprise of you everything on the way."

Holmes gave the man a queer look and said, "Did Mr. Hughes relay to you his overture for my assistance? It was he who had sent me the telegram asking for help in the matter, yet it is an officer of the law who whisks us off to our destination."

"Truth be told, Mr. Holmes, had he not contacted you, I would have. This whole thing has got us all tied up in knots. Mr. Hughes saw us floundering, which I am embarrassed to admit, and I think he overheard me mention your name. Well, he beat me to the punch. When he told me he'd contacted you, I offered to pick you up. Come, I will explain the whole matter on the drive. We should be at the hotel in less than an hour."

As we made our way to Witney Holmes rested his chin on his chest, closed his eyes introspectively, and laced his fingers while Mear relayed to us all relevant information.

"Mr. Francis Erdley," he began, "is a textile merchant, one of the biggest in France. He has been living in Calais for some twenty-five years but was born and raised in Shrewsbury. His younger sister, Beatrice, to whom he is very close, still lives there in their childhood home. Chronic illness and melancholy always prevented her from joining her brother in France, which was often offered, from what I hear, but never accepted. It seems, she was considering finally selling the home and joining her brother, but a potential suitor was vying hard for her affections and to convince her to stay. Erdley was on his way to see her when this unfortunate incident happened."

"You seem to know much about Mr. Erdley's habits and history," my friend noted.

The chief constable smiled, "Part of what I know is from being born and raised in Witney and part is from interviewing his sons who always accompany him. You see, Erdley comes through here every summer on his way to Shrewsbury. A man of habits, he is. Stays at the same hotel and in the same room. Everyone knows or has at least heard of him. He's been doing this since his sons were but children, and they are both strapping young men now—well, at least one is. They always timed their arrival for when the circus came to town, and he would take his sons to see the shows before heading up to see his sister. Ah, but it's been years since Witney's seen the likes of a circus since The Fuller

Brothers Show shut down, and his sons are too old to care besides. Now, they stay but a night, two at most, then are gone like the wind. Three weeks later, they come through once again, catch the train in Oxford, and that is the last we see of them until the next summer."

Although Mear could not recognize it, I have been around my friend too long not to notice the subtle change in Holmes's aquiline features. Something had piqued his interest, yet he did not seem to feel the need to divulge anything presently.

Without rousing himself, Holmes asked, "Who is this potential suitor?"

"A Benny McElwee. He is a blacksmith and a widower. We have dispatched constables in Shrewsbury to question him for obvious reasons. We have not yet heard back in that endeavor."

He turned to me. "Depending on what we find in Witney, Watson, we may have to travel to Shrewsbury."

"And me without my overnight bag," I replied sourly.

"It will not be the first time we have had to make do."

"I have heard no mention of a wife," I commented to Mear.

"She died not too many years after the youngest boy was born, and Mr. Erdley never remarried. I suppose he's got enough to keep him busy with his business and family."

"Please tell me, Constable Mear," Holmes went on, "what are the circumstances around the guarded room? That seems most unusual."

Mear shrugged. "That was at the request of the hotel owner, Mr. Hughes. When Mr. Erdley refused to put the necklace, which he had purchased as a gift for his sister, into a hotel safe, Mr. Hughes insisted extra security be utilized. He employed two off-duty constables at his own expense. He apparently did not feel safe with the necklace not locked away and took this measure to protect himself of liability should anything happen. Erdley was not happy but acquiesced in the end at his youngest son's behest."

"A shrewd move on Mr. Hughes' part," Holmes quipped.

"Yet a strange request, nonetheless," replied Mear. "Erdley always brings along extravagances on which to lavish his sister, who I believe saved him from drowning as a young boy. He brings her Jade from the Orient, leopard skin rugs from safari, fine French wine and the such. Until now, no precautions have ever been taken or needed, for there has never even been an attempt at separating the man from his finery in all these years. Now, maybe it is due to Mr. Hughes' newness as owner of the hotel—a little over a year—and his *anxious* personality, but he insisted on the safeguards."

"Was Mr. Hughes made aware of this ritual of indulgences?" Holmes asked.

"I am sure Erdley made him aware, but it did no good. He was adamant. Hughes is a nice enough fellow but a bit tightly wound."

I asked, "Who found the man dead?"

"His eldest son Jack who'd had the last watch outside his father's door. At seven, he knocked on the door to rouse his father to no avail. Pounding got no reply. Jack finally went down to the front desk to get a spare key. Once inside, Jack found his father with a mortal wound to his head. The weapon, a brass lamp from the nightstand, lay on the floor beside the bed. He is quite beside himself and can't for the life of him figure out how it could have happened. You see, Mr. Holmes, that is the mystery of it all. The room is on the fourth floor of the hotel, and the only possibilities of entry and exit are the room door or a small balcony overlooking the main street. But even the French doors to the balcony were still locked from the inside. And with someone watching the street and another on the roof, there was no opportunity for someone to even climb a rope to the balcony and gain entry that way."

The Chief Constable sighed heavily. There was desperation in his voice when he, at last, said, "We have exhausted every avenue, yet a man is dead and a valuable necklace missing. That is where you come in, Mr. Holmes."

Holmes knitted his brows. "You trust the word of those put in charge of this little endeavor? It could well be, in fact likely, that one of the individuals entrusted as sentry was the culprit."

"Constable Jones is the senior constable in Witney, twenty years of exemplary service, and as far as I am concerned is above reproach. He is a consummate officer of the law. He is willing to swear under oath that the few hours he was on watch nothing of import happened."

"Many a perjurious oath has been uttered before," said Holmes. "Especially when the acquisition of wealth was involved."

"That leaves the son, Jack," I replied. "There has to be something there."

Mear replied, "I would tend to agree, though I am having a hard time with motive. Erdley could be a kind man, well enough, but he could hate with equal measure. I have seen him dote on Jack as his oldest and closest son, but I have also seen him belittled and scolded unmercifully. He is harder on Jack than the younger son, George, but I believe that is because the business will eventually pass to him. George, on the other hand…well, George is more ignored than anything."

Holmes then asked, "And what of the sentries on the roof and street below?

Mear replied, "Constable Archer on the roof, and George Erdley on the street below, walking the length to the crossing streets and back, which with a regular gate would take four minutes, end to end; we timed it."

Holmes was quiet a long moment then finally said, "Thank you. This will give me some data on which to ruminate. Let me dwell on these facts for a time in silence. When we reach Witney, and I can see things for myself, perhaps some light can be shed on this matter of murder, and although it is but little consolation, the sister may yet receive the object of affection from her now late brother."

. . . .

We finally arrived at the King's Lion Hotel. Holmes engaged the constable driving the wagon for a brief, hushed conversation as I eyed a smallish, slender, dark-haired gentleman who gave a nervous smile as he crossed the street to join us. He was well-dressed, yet there was something about him, about the shape of his face that made him look, well…odd, that I think he tried to hide with his full-feather attire. He gave all of us hardy handshakes as Holmes rejoined Mear and me on the sidewalk.

"Thank the heavens you have come, Mr. Holmes!" said he. "This travesty will yet be avenged. Oh, thank the heavens!"

"I am more than happy to help any way I can, Mr. Hughes," Holmes offered.

The man laughed in amazement, "Ha, here only but a moment, and you are already putting your magnificent powers of deduction to use. You are right, I am he but how—"

"Who else could you be?" Holmes cut in, "I can easily spot a suit tailored at Savile Road in London, such as what a fine hotelier would wear; and since you have already telegrammed asking for help, who else would be greeting us so loquaciously?"

Hughes was about to reply, but Mear cut him off, "We shall keep you apprised of any findings, Mr. Hughes, I assure you." Turning to Holmes he then said, "If you would follow me, I shall show you the room."

"I shall also like to see the roof as well."

"Of course."

Hughes grabbed my friend by the cuff of his frock coat, "If you need to see me, Mr. Holmes, I shall be in my office across the street at the Wurthing Park Hotel."

"You own both hotels?"

Rather boastfully, the man replied, "Why yes, I do. My office is on the fourth floor. Come up at your leisure or have a steward come fetch me if you need my assistance with anything. *Anything.*"

"I am quite sure we shall be speaking again shortly."

We walked up the four flights of stairs and past a sentried constable into room 427. It was a luxurious suite with an ample living area and comfortable accoutrements. Locked French doors were centered along the far wall with an adjacent archway on the right which led into the bedroom.

Holmes inspected the room as we slowly made our way across. Nothing seemed to catch his eye, however, he paid most peculiar attention to the carpeting as we walked. "The pile is too short and too new from which to glean any useful information," said he, "and too many footprints have covered any relevant ones."

He then stopped at the French doors. They were indeed locked with a hook and eye latch. He pulled on the doors. They gave only minimally. He then shook the door with a bit more violence. Still, the lock held.

"Surely, someone using that much force would have been heard," said I.

"You are correct, Watson. And even with such rugged testing, the lock held."

He unlocked the door, and the three of us stepped out onto a balcony stretching out roughly five feet from the hotel's exterior wall and was about eight feet in width. Across the street was the building's mirror image, the Wurthing Park Hotel. Resting over the slightly bent, wrought-iron railing in front of us was a small, decorative rug with fringed edges. Its outline could be seen on the stone flooring of the balcony at our feet. Holmes then looked along the hotel front. To his left and right, for the length of the hotel, every room on the fourth floor had a balcony facing the street; however, this balcony was the only one whose rug was not in its rightful place.

"Mear, do you happen to know why this rug is placed over the railing and not where it should be?"

"According to Hughes, to which I can attest, these hotels line a very busy thoroughfare with a multitude of carriages and carts coming and going and kicking up earth. Since it has been very dry and dusty of late, he instructed the staff to pull up the rugs in the evening while the patrons are at dinner and beat the dust from the rugs. Any overly soiled ones are taken and washed. Those that are not washed are left to hang to further help in ridding them of their muck. Then in the morning, they replace the rugs on the balcony floor while the patrons are breakfasting. This one for obvious reasons has not been replaced yet, unlike the others on this floor."

It seemed to me an odd request. "I would be much more concerned with mud and other excrements being tracked in through the hotel room door."

"Yes, me as well," replied Mear. "Hughes' reply was that he replaced all the carpeting in every room on this floor but not the hallways. He didn't care that the hall carpeting got sullied because it was being replaced in September. Any detritus brought in from outside would have already been scuffed off the shoe walking down the carpeted hallway. Standing out on a dirty and dusty balcony though..."

Holmes then said, "Let us now see the bedroom. Chief constable, please lead the way."

As Mear led us from the balcony, I noticed from the corner of my eye, Holmes picked up something from the balcony floor and placed it in his pocket. It looked to be a piece of thread possibly from the fringing of the draped mat. I knew better than to ask. If Holmes has anything akin to a deficiency it is his love of the dramatic. He is like a magician who seeks the look of awe upon the faces of his audience with a splendidly completed act of prestidigitation. I have learned with due diligence he will take me into his confidence; but until that penultimate point, I must be satisfied with my role as a silent partner.

Mear next showed us the bedroom. It was large, clean, and sparsely adorned, save a bed, nightstand and a wardrobe at the far end. A wall clock hung on one wall, while a large painting hung on the other. The room appeared undisturbed everywhere except the left side of the bed and the nightstand. Mr. Erdley had already been taken away, but a ruffled area of the bed and a bloodstained pillow revealed where he had been sleeping when the blow struck. The lamp, consisting of a long, sculpted brass neck with a heavy, round, crystal base still lay on the floor. Splattered blood sullied one side. The drawer of the nightstand protruded, opened approximately half-way.

Mear spoke up as Holmes took in the room with quick yet intense glances, "I have left the room exactly as we found it."

"I applaud you on your diligence," He replied in a half-hearted tone as he studied the scene. "Yet one of the most important pieces has been taken: the body."

"Leaving it in this heat for any extended period was not in anyone's best interest. We had the body taken to Oxford for a post-mortem. It is being performed as we speak, but the cause of death was obvious."

Holmes went to the nightstand and gently closed then reopened the drawer. It squeaked and scratched, wood upon wood, as he pulled it out. "This is the reason why it became necessary to kill Mr. Erdley. Only the soundest of sleepers would not have awakened upon hearing that drawer being opened. No doubt, the necklace was stored within where its owner could keep a close watch on it. When the sound disturbed his slumber, the intruder grabbed what was nearest him to silence Mr. Erdley."

"So far, our routes run parallel, Mr. Holmes. We surmised as much ourselves."

Holmes looked around the room and said to himself quietly, "Yes, but how did he gain entry then leave undetected?"

Next, he began to knock on the walls. All seemed solid.

My friend then opened the wardrobe and inspected Mr. Erdley's suits. I could have sworn I saw him sniffing the air like a dog as he did so. Closing it, Holmes then pulled out and looked behind the wardrobe then crawled across the floor on hands and knees, going over any minutia he happened upon. Having finally satisfied himself that there was nothing left to gain on the floor, Holmes finally regained his height and said, "I should like to see the roof next."

We ascended to the roof, and as Mear opened the door, he said, "There wasn't much to look at up here, Mr. Holmes. Archer, just like Jones, swears it was an uneventful night. He saw nothing, as would be expected."

Holmes waved the statement off as he stepped out onto the flat rooftop, "That which is ignored by others happens to be what I most readily observe."

There was a three-foot parapet around the perimeter of the building. Holmes, with his usual, focused observation, studied the roof in all directions, as he made his way to the front. We followed behind waiting for any revelations.

"One set of footprints from the door to the ledge and back; he was alone."

Holmes then looked over the edge. "Just above and to the right of Erdley's balcony two floors down. Judging by the cigarette remnants, this is where Archer spent most of his time."

He then pointed to more prints along the wall. "This is where he paced, several sets, overlapping." He then followed them. Near the end of the building, he stopped. "It seems constable Archer spent some time here, as well. The track is muddled from standing for some period, and there are several more cigarette butts in this location."

Holmes looked up and scanned the area around, and something across the street caught his eye. "Hullo, what is this? Do you not see the window across the way with its curtains open? And all others are drawn?"

"I do," Mear said. "I fail to see—"

"But I do not," Holmes cut in. "There is more up here than meets the eye."

Holmes then followed the steps back to their place above Erdley's room. "I counted my footsteps, and based on my stride, it is roughly one-hundred seventy feet from here to where Archer turned and came back."

"Is that significant?" Mear asked.

"It could be. We shall see if and where that bit of data fits at a later time. And it seems here," Holmes then added, pointing to a disturbed area on the ground, "that Archer got bored with his duty and sat down, back against the wall, and fell asleep."

"How could you know he fell asleep?" I asked.

"Because, Watson, there are no cigarette butts here. If he remained awake, based on his previous actions, he would have continued to smoke."

Mear scratched his head, dumbfounded. "But Mr. Holmes, I just don't understand where this is all leading."

"Nor do I," my friend replied. "Not yet, though there is an intriguing theory that I feel I must test."

I could almost see those great wheels turning in his mind, as he then turned and hurried to the roof door. "Come, Watson, I must speak to the desk clerk at the hotel across the street briefly then see Mr. Hughes. Mear, if you would be so kind, gather the two constables and the two sons and have them wait outside Erdley's room. I shan't be but a moment, then I wish to talk to them individually. I would also like you standing by with a few of your men. You may be needed shortly."

We rushed across the street to the Wurthing Park Hotel. Upon entering, Holmes spotted the reception area and strolled up to the clerk. "Excuse me, could you tell me if anyone is staying in Room 548?"

The clerk, a young, clean-cut man checked his ledger. "No sir, no one is currently staying in that room. In fact, all rooms in that wing are empty. A bit slow, we are, at the moment. Would you fancy it? It is quite a nice accommodation."

Holmes smiled cordially, "No. Thank you. Could you give me the room number to Mr. Hughes? He is expecting us. I am Sherlock Holmes, and this is my associate, Dr. Watson."

"Ah yes, he did mention you might be over. Room 428, gentlemen."

We were off again. I could tell Holmes was onto something. He was like a hound on the track of a soon-to-be-caught fox.

As we ascended the stairs, I asked, "What was that all about?"

"I wanted to know if anyone was staying in the room with the open curtains."

"But how could you know it was room 548?"

"These hotels are mirror images of each other in every respect—the balconies on the fourth floor of each, same windows and the spacing between them, same length, same six-story height. I daresay the only difference between them is their respective coats of paint. Knowing that, Watson, means that simple math and knowing that even-numbered rooms are on the right side of the corridor and odd-numbered on the left will tell me the number to that room."

We finally found our destination marked with a large, gold placard that read *Mr. Milton Hughes, Proprietor*. Holmes knocked.

There was a brief silence then came the call from inside, "Come in."

Milton Hughes was sitting behind a large mahogany desk at the far end of the room with French doors leading to the balcony directly at his back, open, letting in the warmth of the day. He rose from his desk and gestured to the seats in front of the desk. "Come, sit. I hope you have good news to tell me regarding this ugly affair."

We sat, and I could not help but notice the piles of stationery, envelopes, and letters alike, strewn about his desk, a long, gold letter opener on top of it all. A spent pipe lay at the other end. His workspace was an antithesis to his dapper, perfectly groomed attire.

"I am still a bit in the dark on the matter," Holmes said, "but I am making some headway. I shall resume my investigation shortly but came to inform you that you have, or should say *had,* an interloper in room 548."

"Does this somehow tie into Mr. Erdley's murder?" he asked.

"I do not believe in coincidences, Mr. Hughes. I believe someone in that room distracted the guard on the roof, and I believe the distraction was intentional."

He looked from one to the other of us. "Distraction? I apologize Mr. Holmes, but your thinking in this has far outpaced mine. I am in the dark as to what you mean."

"Sometime during Constable Archer's sentry on the rooftop, he happened upon someone in a room across the street and one floor down at the far end, which your desk clerk was kind enough to divulge was an area of Wurthing Park currently unoccupied. Archer noticed this person because the window curtains were open. I surmise this person to be a woman, for who else but the fairer sex would a man stop in his normal course of duties to watch?"

Hughes began to rise, "Well, we shall put a stop to that. Come, let's see if the freeloader is still using the room."

Holmes put up a hand and motioned for Hughes to sit back down. "I do not think you will find anyone there at present, so the effort would be a wasted one, and my efforts are too precious to waste. That was only part of the reason I came over. I wanted to see if you would allow me a different view of Erdley's balcony. I need a wider view than that which I am getting currently with my feet on the crime scene."

Holmes rose from his seat and gestured toward the balcony doors. "May I?"

Hughes and I got up from our chairs simultaneously as he said, "Of course, of course. Please do."

We all went outside.

Holmes said, "Yours is the perfect vantage point for what I want to see, being directly across the street from his balcony." He scanned the top of the building across the street then leaned over the railing and looked at the street below and in both directions, taking in everything in long, intense gazes.

Hughes whispered to me as Holmes studied his canvas, "What do you think he is looking for?"

I replied quietly, "With Sherlock Holmes, every bit of minutia is but a piece to a puzzle no one else seems to know how to put together…In other words, I have no idea."

When Holmes was done, he turned and walked back inside, remarking to Hughes as he passed, "Your railing is slightly bent. I would have that repaired before it becomes a hazard."

"Oh yes," Hughes replied as we followed Holmes back into the office. "Already noted—that one and a few others, I must admit. I bought these hotels at a bargain, but the consternation of it all is the amount of money needed to bring them back to respectability."

As Holmes passed the disheveled desk, some bit of stationary caught his eye. "I see an envelope with a French postmark."

"Ah, yes, you would notice that, wouldn't you? Well, at present, I am in negotiations with a small hotel in Dunkirk. No resting on any laurels for this hotelier."

"Going international, I see," said I.

He smiled weakly. "Trying to. It is a sobering affair, to say the least. I have been told that I am a bit, shall we say, excitable. My wife says I do not have the fortitude to take on such endeavors. However, the more she says it, the more I try to prove her wrong. But I fear she may be right. They are hard negotiators, the French. They want well more than I think it's worth, and I am deciding now on my next move. Or I was until this morning."

"Well, I wish you luck in your endeavor," I replied.

Holmes spoke up. "I am preparing to interview the constables and Mr. Erdley's sons, with another person of interest possibly afterward. I would like for you to come over, if you would, in one hour, and I will apprise you on what I've found thus far."

"Another person?" Hughes asked.

"Yes, another suspect was brought up when Mear apprised us of the situation on the trip from Oxford."

"May I ask who this person is?"

"You may not," was Holmes' curt reply. "One hour. If you are needed sooner, I shall send for you, if that is alright."

"Of course," Hughes nodded in that frazzled way of his, and we took our leave.

. . . .

Holmes spoke to Chief Constable Mear down on the street, momentarily, while I set up Mr. Erdley's room for interviews. When he finally arrived, Holmes sat in a large, leather wingback in the middle of the room, and I had pulled out an armless chair from the writing desk and placed it in front of him. When he was seated, he nodded, and I let the first of the four men inside. It was Archer, the constable from the roof, a fair-haired, balding young man who tried to make up for his sparse top by growing out large tufts of side whiskers. His nervousness was palpable as he sat in the chair in front of Holmes, while I leaned against the writing desk taking in the interrogation.

"Let us cut to the chase, constable. I shall tell you what I know, and you shall fill in the gaps."

"I shall, Mr. Holmes," he said shakily.

"I know you spent some time watching someone through their window across the street. A woman, yes?"

The man nodded.

"Did you recognize her?"

"No sir, Mr. Holmes, though she had her back to me the whole time."

"You never saw her face?"

"No, sir."

"Relay the incident, if you would."

Archer cleared his throat. "Well, I had paced the top of the roof for some time, going over to the far edge and back 'bout every half-hour or so. 'Bout two hours into my watch, that would have been 'round midnight or so, as I made my way over to the far end of the building, this light comes on 'cross the way there. Naturally, I'm curious."

"Naturally," my friend repeated with deprecation.

"Well, this woman proceeds to—undress with her back to the window."

An uncomfortable silence followed. The man seemed embarrassed at the last statement. Holmes bit into the silence with a bit of exasperation, "What was she wearing? What color was her hair? Was she alone? This would be helpful information."

Archer said, clearing his throat once more. "She was wearing a long dress, a nice one too, like she'd been out to a fancy dinner or some such. She had blonde hair, and she was alone as far as I could tell. I saw no one else in the room. After about twenty minutes or so, as she came and went from view in front of the window, the light went out, and I resumed my watch."

He then looked from one to the other of us pleadingly. "It was just a bit of harmless looking. She was right there in front of the window. What was a man supposed to do?

I said, "A gentleman would have looked away."

"And you will swear that this all transpired in roughly twenty-minutes' time?" asked Holmes.

"Maybe five-minutes either side of that, sir, but certainly less than a half-hour."

"And how long were you asleep?"

The man seemed astounded as he looked upon us. "How could you know that?"

Holmes replied, "It is easier for me to just know than it is to explain *how* I know. Please, answer the question."

"I admit I knocked off for another half hour. When I woke, I checked my pocket watch, and it read a hair past one. I got up and resumed my watch."

"So, there was slightly less than an hour where you were negligent in your duties?"

The man shook his head in protest. "If that's how you want to look at it, but let's be honest, Mr. Holmes, no one was on the roof but me, and the prints in the dirt and muck up there prove that. In whatever manner Mr. Erdley met his end, it did not come by the roof."

"One last question, if I may. Did you happen at any point see Mr. Erdley the younger on his similar patrol on the street below?"

"I saw him once or twice, each time it was in the same place. He was 'bout halfway down the street from the front entrance, leaning up against a gaslight reading."

"Letter or book?"

Archer thought a moment. "Couldn't say for certain because I really wasn't paying much attention to him, but if I was forced to guess I'd say it looked like a letter."

"Thank you, that will be all. Could you please have the older Erdley brother come in next?"

Archer nodded, rose from his seat, and left the room in quickstep, a mixture of fear and relief awash on his face.

"What do you make of him?" I asked in a hushed tone in the interim.

"Incompetent. That is all I will say at present, but the list of adjectives may yet grow."

Next was Jack Erdley. He was a tall, muscular young man with short brown hair and a mustache. He looked tired and forlorn with thick red welts about both eyes. He took his seat across from Holmes and sighed heavily.

Holmes started things off. "I won't take up too much of your time, Mr. Erdley. I am sorry for your loss."

"Thank you," he replied with a sniffle.

"You are the one who found your father, is that correct?"

"Yes, sir, Mr. Holmes. When my father would not rouse and unlock the door, I went and fetched another key from the desk clerk."

The man had a crisp, baritone voice with no French roll of the *R's;* he had a distinctly British tone. For one born and raised in France, I would have expected a more French dialect. I relayed that thought aloud.

"My mother," he replied, "was from Birmingham and didn't care much for the French language or lifestyle. We only spoke it when we had to and never at home. Though not fluent, I do speak it well when the need arises."

Shooting me an agitated look, Holmes regained his foothold in the questioning and went on, "So you knew where to find the extra key?"

"I knew to whom I should go for the extra key, not where it was located."

"I have been told that your father could be rather—short with you. Is that a correct assessment of your relationship?"

"If you are asking if my father could be cross with me, the answer would be yes. What good father wouldn't be? I am in line to take over a rather large company with many people relying on its proper running for their livelihood, and there have been times where my immaturity has gotten the better of me. I am grateful that I had a father who corrected my errors. I am a better man for it. But let me say this, Mr. Holmes, it was never done maliciously, and I never took it as such. He was a good man and a good father. Better than most."

Holmes bowed his head slightly. "I apologize for the unintended implication." Then, with brow askew, Holmes added, "Would your younger brother feel the same way?"

Jack Erdley squirmed uncomfortably in his seat. "You will have to ask him that question yourself. I am not my brother's keeper."

"And I shall, shortly. That is all for now. Thank you. Could you ask the constable who was on duty before you to come in next, please?"

"He seemed very upset about his father," said I. "Despite the public remonstrations of the lad, I would wager they were very close. I highly doubt it was him."

He gave me a wry smile and said, "That is why I like having you with me, Watson. "You always point me to the right path by your wrong deductions."

"Do you honestly think it was him?"

"I think I shall keep my intimations to myself at present. I haven't yet spoken to all who need spoken to. It is possible my theory may change between now and then."

The next man in was Constable Jones. He was a middle-aged, barrel-chested man with a close-shaved head and whiskers. His blue eyes and wide smile made him out to be a cheerful fellow as he greeted us and sat in the chair across from Holmes.

Holmes started, "Constable, you had the first shift which began about ten last evening, correct?"

"Yes, sir, Mr. Holmes. It was 10:12 by my pocket watch. Mr. Erdley, after some mumblings about a big waste of time, closed and locked the door. I even checked it after I heard the lock engage." He looked over at me and with a stern nod said, "I take my job seriously, I do."

"Not serious—"

"And your help in this matter is greatly appreciated, both in your duty last night and now," I remarked loudly, cutting off what was sure to be a sarcastic rebuttal by Holmes.

I scowled at Holmes when the constable looked away.

My friend proceeded. "You stayed for only part of your shift before being replaced by the older Erdley brother, yet everyone else had an all-night shift. Why would that be?"

"I was asked to stay the whole night, but the older Erdley boy offered to split the night with me, as my wife is expecting our first, and she is due soon. I know what you must be thinking with me at my age being a father for the first time, but my wife is a bit younger than me, and we've been trying with no luck for a long time. God finally smiled on us, and I'll take a son at any age." He then knocked on the wood of the chair, I assumed for luck. He continued, "Little George Erdley, who'd been walking up and down the street, came up and told me that he stopped a man on the street who was coming to get me, for my wife was in labor. He told me he would fetch his brother to finish the watch, and I was to go."

Tapping his fingers on the armrest as he thought, Holmes then asked, "Pray tell, did you leave the hotel through the front doors?"

"No sir, Mr. Holmes. I left out a back door by the kitchen since our house is behind the hotel and four streets west."

Holmes was silent, momentarily, then began again. "And, you wouldn't know for how long the room door was left unattended before Jack Erdley arrived?"

"It wasn't left unattended, Mr. Holmes. I waited until George Erdley came back with his brother before I left. Like I said, I take my job seriously and would never have left that door unattended. I figured I wouldn't miss much in the five minutes it took to fetch his brother."

"So, are you a new father yet?" I asked.

The man wrinkled his brow. "That's the thing, sir. When I got home, my wife wasn't in any labor at all and didn't know anything about telling anyone to come fetch me. Well, that worried my wife, so I stayed home with her, knowing that Jack Erdley had taken my place."

After a few moments' contemplation, eyes closed, fingers crossed, Holmes reanimated and said, "Thank you, Constable Jones, that will be all. Please send in Erdley the Younger next.

George Erdley was a bit younger than his brother, barely over twenty, and quite frankly seemed a polar opposite. He was slightly built with long, straight, black hair in the French style that covered his ears and dark close-set eyes. He was emotionless and sat quietly in the seat opposite Holmes.

My friend said nothing at first and just eyed the young man curiously. This unnerved him for he began to fidget in his seat and pushed back the long hair from his ears, momentarily, then arranged it back.

"You told Constable Jones," Holmes began, "that a man came looking for him to tell him his wife was about to give birth, is that correct?"

"Yes," was his curt answer.

"Can you describe this man?"

"Not really. I met him at the far corner of the street. There were no streetlamps there, so he was but a shadow as we spoke. I asked him where he was going, and the man said he was on his way to fetch the constable at the hotel because his wife was having a baby. I told him to go tell the constable's wife that he was on his way, and I'd run up to tell him because I knew where he was."

"And you went straight up and relayed the news to Constable Jones?"

"Without delay," he replied.

"Just a few more questions, if I may. Did you see anyone or anything unusual in the hotel across the street at around midnight?"

George Erdley replied without hesitation, "No, should I have?"

Holmes didn't answer the question. Instead, he asked, "What were you reading under the streetlamp? The constable on the roof mentioned seeing you reading."

"A letter."

"From whom?"

The young man momentarily looked down at his feet then re-engaged Holmes. "A—she's a female acquaintance. A friend from back home. She wrote me a letter before we left Calais. When I get lonely, I pull it out and read it." He stopped then added hastily, "I know it's a silly notion, sir, but I assure you, I am not a lovesick child. We were going to be away only a month, but she was insistent on giving me the letter to read while apart.

"Why did you not read it out in front of the hotel? There is more light coming from the hotel lobby and with the streetlamp there, surely that would have afforded you more light with which to read your *billet-doux*."

He seemed unsure of what to say. At last, he remarked, "The lamp outside the hotel does not work, and I did not wish any prying eyes see me reading instead of walking my post."

"Would your father have been upset with you, if he found out you had not followed instruction?"

George Erdely chortled. "I doubt my *father* would have cared one way or another."

"Do you have this letter on you presently?"

The young man's face became flushed. "I do not. It is—it is in my room, and I do not wish for someone I do not know to read intimacies meant for me."

Sherlock Holmes was about to remark when there came an insistent knock at the door. Our constable/driver entered. "A note for you, Mr. Holmes."

"Thank you," he said, taking the paper. A thin, wide grin creased his features as he read. "Bravo, Mrs. Hudson! This is exactly as I had construed." To the constable, he then said, "Please have the other three gentlemen come back into the room. Then please have Chief Constable Mear ask for Mr. Hughes to join us. He will no doubt like to hear what I have found out. Then, tell Mear to do as I had instructed him earlier."

The officer nodded then left as quickly as he came.

In short order, the four men were back inside the room with Mr. Hughes joining us. They sat and stared at one another in silence, each seeming to size the other up for guilt. Hughes looked them all over with a somewhat confused look upon his face, as though somehow not believing any of the men could be the culprit.

Finally, Chief Constable Mear barged through the door. He had a look of amazement upon his face. "I don't know how you knew Mr. Holmes, but by George you hit it square on. Just where you said it would be." He then marched over to Milton Hughes and grabbed him by the arm. "I am arresting you for the murder of Francis Erdley."

The man looked around astonished. "Why, this is preposterous! How on earth could *I* have been the murderer?"

I must readily admit that I, for the life of me, could not figure out how Holmes had come to such an outlandish conclusion.

Holmes spoke up, regarding Mr. Hughes directly. "Let me tell the sequence of events, and you can tell me where I have strayed from the path of fact. Nodding to me, he asked, "Do you remember, Watson, me telling you that the name Milton Hughes sounded familiar to me?"

"I do," said I. "I remarked to you that you should look the name up in your index, but we would then miss the train."

"Yes, well looking up that name would have been fruitless. But Mear unwittingly gave me a name that my index would have had—the Fuller Brothers' Circus. When we got to town, I had a constable send a telegram to Mrs. Hudson, who returned the telegram just now, relaying everything I had on my index card. It was a case I was very interested in some years back. It involved the murder of one of the owners, Gerald Fuller in Ipswich. It was a murder never solved. I had followed the investigation closely for a while and was about to insert myself into it when the police began running out of leads. Unfortunately, some fortuitous events took me to Switzerland, and I was forced to drop my interest in the case. You see, I believed, but it was never proven, that his half-brother and co-owner was the murderer."

"And that was Milton Hughes," I finished.

"I was an innocent man then, and I am innocent now," Hughes resounded. "Just because I was part of a murder investigation some six years ago, does not make me a murderer now. And you have yet to mention how this was pulled off. One door was guarded, the other locked, and people on the roof and street. How could I have done it without being seen?"

"I will get to that point shortly. Please, let us set this out in order." Holmes continued as he paced the floor. "If you were going to pull this off, you needed an accomplice, and he took the form of George Erdley."

Now, it was George Erdley's turn to look surprised.

"Why would the boy help in the murder of his father?" I asked.

"You are incorrect on two points, Watson. It was not meant initially to be a murder, only a robbery. Also, George Erdley is not Francis Erdley's son. He is Milton Hughes'."

Hughes glared at Holmes, and George Erdley only stared at his feet.

"And what makes you think the boy is mine?" Hughes asked smugly.

"It is quite easy. You both have the same facial anomaly. You make others cast their gaze elsewhere by your dapper appearance. Your son chooses only to conceal it with his long hair. When he briefly rearranged his hair as we spoke, it was quite obvious. Both of you were born with your right ear considerably lower than your left. A hereditary trait, no doubt."

Looking upon Jack Erdley, Holmes then said, "Your father knew the boy was not his, and that is why he paid so little attention to George."

Jack nodded. "On one of our first trips to see Aunt Bea, my father and mother had a row after having taken me to see the circus. It started over dinner, and they both liked their wine, so it was probably alcohol-induced, whatever it was about. She stormed out and returned late that evening. They made up the next day, but in that time away, she'd had a…dalliance with another man. My dad was heartbroken after she admitted her subsequent pregnancy and that the baby wasn't his. Our mother would die within two years of George's birth, overcome with the guilt of her indiscretion. We never knew who his father was."

"Well, you do now," Holmes continued in that almost emotionless way he can sometimes have. "Many regrettable things are done in anger, and when alcohol is involved the ramifications are quite often more dire."

Hughes protested. "Abnormalities of all sorts are common to most folks. There is no way it can ever be proven that George Erdley is my son. Ask his mother who the father is. Oh, wait. You can't. She is dead."

Nodding to Mear, Holmes asked, "Did you bring the implements?"

"They are out in the hallway. Shall I retrieve them?"

"Yes, now would be a good time."

Mear brought forth a long, thick length of rope. Attached to one end was a large two-pronged hook. Along with it, he produced three long poles that could be attached at the ends. At the end of one pole was a small bifurcation in the shape of a *Y*. "They were found in a utility closet in the hallway, just down from Hughes' office."

Holmes proceeded. "Either the poles were already fastened together and handed to George Erdley through the front doors of the Wurthing Park Hotel, which is the more likely scenario, or perhaps he fastened the poles together himself outside. He then placed the hooked end of the rope in the notch of the long pole and hoisted it up and hooked it onto the railing padded with the balcony mat so as to avoid any metallic clanking. The other end was already attached to a winch on Hughes' balcony, which is directly across the street."

"I left the winch in the utility closet due to its bulky weight," Mear interrupted.

"George Erdley then placed the implements back inside the Wurthing hotel and went up to his father's room to tell Jones of the imminent birth of his son. It was during this anxious time and the switch of sentries from Jones to Jack Erdley that the murder and robbery took place."

"He shimmied along the rope to the other side?" I asked.

"No, Watson. Along with being a co-owner of the circus, Milton Hughes was also an accomplished tight-rope walker. He was part of the show. Did you not notice that both wrought-iron railings across from each other were bent outward? Hughes managed to disfigure them, however slightly, on his walk over and back."

"You cannot prove any of that," Hughes retorted. Pointing to the rope and poles, he continued, "Those are just old trinkets, fond memories I took with me when the Circus folded from all the bad publicity. You still haven't hinted as to how I gained access to a locked room."

"Mear?" Holmes called out.

Mear produced the golden letter opener, the one I remembered from Hughes' desk and handed it to Holmes.

"I shall show you how the door was unlocked and relocked. Watson, would you be so kind as to lock the French doors behind me, please?"

We both walked over to the doors, and Holmes stepped out onto the balcony. I closed the doors and locked them. As soon as I stepped away, the doors bent in slightly, just enough to put a sliver of an opening between them, and Holmes stuck the thin blade of the letter opener into that gap and ran it upwards, pushing the hook out of the eye latch.

"That is step one," said I. "What about the much harder relocking of the door?"

"It is not as impossible as one would think." He then produced the long thread he had picked up from the balcony floor earlier. He proceeded to tie one end around the hook then fed the string through the eye latch. Keeping ahold of the string, Holmes then slowly closed the door. Then, from the other side, he gently pulled the string, and the hook fell onto the opening of the eye latch. With one harder tug, it re-latched. With a second, firm yank, the string was pulled free from the hook and pulled outside.

I was, quite frankly, amazed.

I opened the doors and let my friend back in.

"That," he said, "is how you unlock and re-lock a hook and eye latch lock. This all happened while Constable Archer was watching Hughes' wife undress in the hotel room across the street to keep him away from the area while the whole event transpired."

Hughes began to clap. "Bravo, Mr. Holmes, but there is one problem: without the necklace, all this is but conjecture. It all fits, but there is no proof the murder and robbery happened that way at all. In fact, I would wager most would think it a quite wild theory."

Holmes gave Mear a look, and Mear nodded slightly in return. "We had men placed at the train stations in Oxford and Yarnton," Mear began. "We snared her while catching the 4:10 to York in Oxford. Guess what we found on her? A beautiful ruby necklace."

Holmes said, "As long as there was no proof, you knew no one would ultimately be charged in this case. So, you had your wife leave with the necklace for safekeeping until you could meet up with her and exchange it on the black market for cash."

Turning to Archer, Holmes added, "His wife is the woman you saw in the window."

"It could not have been," Archer rejoined. "I know Mrs. Hughes. She is not blonde. She has brown hair."

"You did not recognize her because of her use of a wig. It was her fear of identification that kept her face from the window."

Turning back to Hughes, Holmes said satisfactorily, "Am I missing anything, Mr. Hughes? I believe I have produced methods and proof. That should suffice to see you in a noose."

As more constables came into the room, Hughes smiled and nodded in acquiescence to Holmes. "If you would have been in my circus, I could have made you a rich man with that great brain of yours."

"Then I would have been betraying my master for thirty pieces of silver, and that is something I shall never do."

As Hughes and George Erdley were led out of the room by constables, Jack Erdley came up and shook Sherlock Holmes' hand. "Thank you for bringing that murderous letch to light, Mr. Holmes. It saddens me to think my brother had a hand in this black affair, but I am glad that justice shall be served."

"For all but your brother," was his reply. "He had no hand in how he was created. If he had been treated differently by those closest to him, this ordeal may never have presented itself."

"There will be much guilt that I shall have to live with," said Jack mournfully.

"What will you do now?" I asked the young man.

"I have some sad news to depart to my aunt. I shall stay with her just as my father would have done. But I suspect I shall cut the visit short. There is a burial to prepare for and a business that will need an Erdley hand to operate. I truly hope I am ready."

I put a hand on his shoulder. "I'm sure you will do just fine."

When we were finally alone on the train back to London. I engaged my friend. "I just do not understand what a well-to-do hotelier would need with a necklace. Do you think he was trying to use it to get extra capital to buy that hotel in France?"

"No, Watson. He was not buying a hotel in France. That was a cover for his correspondence with his son unless the hotel's name was George. Even upside down and partially covered, I can read French. That letter George was reading under the lamp post, certainly now destroyed, more than likely had the intended plan and George's part in it. During their correspondence, George must have made mention of the valuable necklace, and that started Hughes' evil mind turning. Circus performers have a unique set of skills that would come in handy should they decide to take a more nefarious turn in life. I happened to see several bills strewn across that calamity of a desk of his. My guess would be that the hotels were losing money, and he saw the necklace as a way to pay off some of his many delinquent bills. He had killed once and avoided the docks. When Erdley woke during the robbery, it was an easier step this time to murder."

"I wonder how Hughes and George Erdley ever came to realize their relationship. Do you think it was the ears?"

"You saw them, Watson. Maybe apart, people would not notice the similarity. But it was quite easy to see with the two of them together that there were too many featural similarities to come to any other conclusion. I suspect once Hughes realized his brief interlude with Mrs. Erdley created an offspring, he approached the young man, told him the details, and struck up a long-distance relationship. It is also quite possible Hughes knew all along that George was his son and bought the hotels as a way to see his son, even if only once a year."

"I shook my head. "I don't understand why he even contacted you at all. He all but signed his own death warrant by doing so."

"When he overheard Mear contemplating bringing me in, he usurped the police and contacted me himself." With a flair of his hand, he added. "Who would think to believe the one employing my services to find the murderer would, in fact, be the murderer. Friends close, Watson, and enemies closer."

"Little did he know…" I started.

"Yes, Watson," came the reply with a smile, "little did he know…"

The End

Mass Murder

(Previously published in MX Publishing's Book of New Sherlock Holmes Stories)

1901 was a year bookended by loss. The country lost its queen in the beginning weeks of the year, and Holmes and I lost a dear friend on the last day of December. We were, however, lucky enough to have had the pleasure of spending some time with him before his death. Yet life does not sit idle as you have your last moments together. It goes on in all its glory and all its indignity. It is these indignities of life with which my friend Sherlock Holmes so competently deals, and he must deal with them regardless of the circumstance or time in which they arise. So, it should not surprise the reader which path Holmes took when presented with such a dilemma during a time he would rather have spent with a sick friend.

As I stood waiting for the slowing train to stop, I could not help but feel a sense of relief that Holmes had finally found some time to pull away from his investigations for a break. I had convinced him to come over to Woodford-Upon-Lea in Essex for some sunshine and cool, fresh air, which had been the climate at the time of the telegram. Now, unfortunately, the blue skies of early October had been replaced by grey, windswept clouds, which constantly dropped their burden with enthusiastic abandon.

I myself had gone two weeks earlier to help a long-time, mutual friend, Phineas Whympenny, convalesce as he recovered from some serious hypertensive issues. It was those issues from which he, unfortunately, never fully recovered.

Holmes had said he would pay a visit once his current affair wrapped up, and I received a telegram the day before that he would be on the morning train.

Shaking hands once he departed the train, I said, "I am glad that you could finally get away, Holmes."

"Once I was sure the broker was stealing his own diamonds, I set Lestrade on that trail to do the work for which he is best suited. It took some time to prove my deductions correct, but alas, here I am. Better late than never. So, is the good Mr. Whympenny recovering sufficiently? I hope he has not taken a similar turn as that of the wonderful weather you promised."

"The weather I communicated was from a week ago," I replied as we retrieved his baggage. "You cannot expect our finicky weather to keep its good humour for any great length of time. And as far as our friend Phin is concerned, he is feeling better now, but he is not yet out of the woods. I fear for the man, but he refuses to change his diet. As you know, Phin is nearing sixty-five, and he was never what one would call *fit*."

"I dare say, Watson, that for an epicurean whose height and circumference are practically interchangeable, fit has *never* been a useful adjective to describe old Phin. It may be that his taste for food has finally taken its toll."

"Yes, but he is as jolly as ever," said I. "A smile never seems far from his face, and he is anxious to see his favourite customer."

"Is he well enough for some oysters and a brace of grouse?" Holmes asked when we climbed into the taxi.

"He is out of bed for short spells a few times a day. I am sure, with some help on our part, he would be willing to boil, bake, sauté, smoke, or pickle just about anything you ask."

. . . . .

Phineas Whympenny's home was the last amongst an assemblage of large, well-kept cottages on Old Oak Lane at the edge of the village. And here, the separation was abrupt between civilization and an expanse of low-rolling farmland and wood. I was pointing out Phin's cottage as we slowed, but Holmes was more interested in the happenings across the street. A constabulary wagon was situated in front of a small, sandstone church. Four officers were at its entrance, one talking, the others listening intently.

"It seems the Church has need of a little law and order," said Holmes as I disembarked with the bags, and he paid the driver.

"I wonder if Phin caught a glimpse of anything," I added. "Maybe he could fill us in on what we missed."

"Or better yet…" Holmes replied as he walked briskly across the street.

I looked at Holmes then to the cottage. I noticed Phin's bulk framed by the parlour window. His massive shoulders bounced as he chuckled, and he waved me off as if to say, *Go join Holmes*.

I smiled at him and shrugged sheepishly. I then put the overnight bags down on the small front porch and joined Holmes on the other side of the street, as he was reading the signage on the front lawn which read *Saint Anne's Catholic Church*.

We were met on the walkway by a young, clean-shaven constable whose forlorn features betrayed a tragedy. "I'm sorry, gentlemen, but Saint Anne's is closed."

"May we inquire as to the reason for its shuttering?" asked Holmes.

"It is a crime scene," said the constable laconically.

With aplomb, my friend replied, "Well, I am Sherlock Holmes, and this is my colleague, Dr. Watson."

"Ah, the famous consulting detective from London," he said in a revelatory tone. "Here on holiday? You missed some nice walking weather by a few days, but I am sure the sun will return if you are patient enough. Or could it be that your deductive powers are more impressive than what the good doctor chronicles, and you were brought to this crime scene by mere instinct."

Looking over the constable's shoulder at the church, ignoring the thin smile of amusement that creased the officer's face, Holmes replied with a bit of veiled sarcasm, "No holiday and no superhuman feats of intellect. I apologize if that revelation lessens your impression of my ability to deduce or my colleague's ability to write. Yet, my arrival was not a fortuitous one. We are here visiting an old friend across the street." He engaged the constable with a cold, direct stare, "And since we are here, would the local authorities have any need of my assistance?"

The constable's smile disappeared at the subtle reproof. He cleared his throat. "Of course, of course." Shaking our hands, the man went on, "I am Constable Milks, Benny Milks. And please, come, let me show you what we have. It's not the usual fare in a village this size, and probably a bit dull for the likes of you, Mr. Holmes, but having the great detective on board will all but ensure the proper outcome."

"What about poor, old Phin?" I asked Holmes. "He has been anxiously awaiting your arrival."

"My plan was for a week's stay, Watson. A few stray moments here and there will not hurt the quality of our company."

"Gentlemen," Constable Milks said as he opened the left side of the double doors. "Please come through this door, as the right is part of the crime scene which I will explain momentarily."

When the constable moved to open the door for us, it was then that I noticed briefly detritus of some sort, possibly stomach contents, upon the entranceway just in front of the right-side door.

We followed Milks into the narthex of the small church. From there we looked out into the nave, consisting of a central aisle and fifteen rows of pews on either side. Each row could accommodate roughly ten people. Directly in front of us, five rows back from the communion railing, a body lay awkwardly, half in the center aisle and half-hidden by a pew. Three more bodies lay at slumped angles, all in the same pew. In front of the altar a priest knelt, head bowed in prayer, with an officer standing over him.

"Instead of just relaying what was said to us, I shall let the priest explain things," Milks said. "I will just say that sometime before the benediction all the attendants became quite ill. A fifth attendant, Miss Mary Holowczak, the housemaid and cook, became ill, as well, but managed to crawl to the door and was halfway through before she retched and collapsed. A neighbor walking his dog saw her there and notified us."

"And she is still alive?" I asked.

"At the moment, but she is in a bad way."

Looking on at the scene like an anxious terrier being held back by a leash, Holmes responded, "I should like to see the bodies, if I may."

Acquiescing with a sweep of his arm, Constable Milks said, "After you, gentlemen."

As we approached the first body lying half in the aisle, Milks offered, "This is Ramsey Montfort. He is Sir Gordon Montfort's eldest child and only son. Sir Montfort is the local squire, whose noble name can be traced all the way back to the Battle of Hastings."

At this, Holmes knelt and examined the body, which was crumpled in a heap upon the floor. The Montfort boy, no more than in his early twenties, was on his stomach, head cocked to the side, arms, and hands at awkward angles. Holmes sniffed around the young man's mouth and examined his clothing.

"The three others here," Milks continued, pointing to the other bodies, "are John Wallace, Harold Harker, and Oliver Warleggan."

They were each slumped over in various positions. There was no visible frothing or vomiting, and I, using my olfactory senses, smelled no bitter almonds or garlic, so my personal opinion was that whatever the poison, it was not arsenic or cyanide.

Somehow knowing my inner thoughts—or more likely seeing me sniff the air—Holmes spoke up, "I do not think it is

Strychnine, either, Watson. My guess is hemlock. It mixes well with wine and other liquids. Depending on the dosage, it could have been administered anytime from breakfast to the blood of Christ."

"I do not see how they could drink and die, and the priest seems to suffer no ill consequence," said I.

Milks spoke up, eyeing the praying priest intently. "He might have put his lips to the chalice, but that does not mean he drank. And his back is turned to the congregants. He could have easily concealed the fact that he did not drink from the cup."

"You think he did it?" I asked

"As you say," Milks responded, "the priest is alive while all others are dead."

"Not quite everyone," Holmes added sagely.

"If the girl survives it will be by luck alone."

As he eyed the priest at the altar, kneeling in prayer while a constable stood over him, Holmes asked in a low voice, almost to himself, "Why would a man in charge of another man's spiritual life so callously take his physical one?" Turning back to Milks, Holmes then asked, "Where was the girl sitting?"

"According to Father Harrison, she was in the next pew behind the men."

"I would like to speak to the priest now, if I may," said my friend.

Milks relieved the constable guarding Father Harrison, and the priest finally stood, regarding the three of us with worry deepening the wrinkles around his weathered yet handsome features.

"This is Sherlock Holmes from London. He would like to talk to you," Milks offered. "I shall be nearby if you need me, gentlemen."

"I—I do not know what to tell you," he said, regarding us. "They were all fine one moment, and the next…" his voice trailed off.

"Come, sit with us in this first pew, here," Holmes suggested with forbearance, "and relay to me the events of the morning."

The three of us sat in the front pew while the officers set about investigating around us.

Holmes took a languid position in the pew, fingers interlaced introspectively, eyes closed, and began, "So, is it the habit of these gentlemen to attend morning Mass?"

Taking out a handkerchief and wiping the copious perspiration from his forehead with a shaking hand, the priest said, "If it weren't for them there would be no morning Mass when I have it. They only come after hunting."

"I am not sure I understand. Please elaborate, and start from the beginning, please."

"All the land around, including the property the church sits on is owned by Sir Gordon Montfort. He gave the land on which the church is built for his son, Ramsey, who converted to Catholicism three years ago. They often come over for meals, and taking breakfast before a hunt has become their habit."

"They breakfasted with you this morning?" Holmes asked.

"Oh yes. Miss Mary makes a big breakfast before every hunt. They and Miss Mary are often my only company." With an earnest smile, he then added, "We are a small congregation at the moment, but we are slowly growing. Most Sundays it is only Ramsey and his four friends and Miss Holowczak—Mary, with but a few others, but on holidays and some holy days of obligation, we are able to get upwards of thirty people for Mass, much to the chagrin of Sir Gordon."

I wrinkled my brow. "I don't think I follow. You just said that Gordon Montfort gave the land the church was built on. Why then would he not wish the church to grow?"

"Sir Gordon is a staunch Anglican and saying he wasn't fond of Catholics would be a severe understatement. He was heartbroken when Ramsey told him he was converting. But Ramsey is his only son, so he usually gets what he wants. I have tried to accentuate what we have in common when we have a chance to converse, but our short dialogues never blossom into any sort of constructive conversation."

"Getting back to this morning," Holmes said with no slight irritation, "did anything unusual happen at breakfast?"

"No, nothing. It was as it has been every other day. Miss Mary came in this morning around five. I know this because I myself arise early and pray in the church, so I was there when I heard her come in through the rectory."

"Does she live nearby?"

"She rents a room five cottages down from the church. She doesn't normally come in that early. Ramsey tells us when the spirit moves him for a hunt, and she arrives accordingly to start on breakfast."

"Of what does your breakfast typically consist?"

"Miss Mary usually has sausage, kidneys, eggs, toast, and marmalade set out for us, along with both coffee and tea. Oh, yes, she also sets out a bowl of czarnina soup for herself and me. I have, over these past several months, taken a liking to eastern European cuisine, and czarnina soup has become one of my favorites. Only she and I eat it, as the others do not think it appetizing. Today was just as any other day, as far as I could discern. We ate, and they went off to hunt."

"Czarnina soup—Mary is Galician?" Holmes asked.

"That is correct."

"Is it your habit to let the help eat meals with you?"

The priest frowned. "I do not consider Miss Mary *help*. This might be her situation, but she is God's creature all the same. She is always welcome at table, especially when it's her meals being consumed."

Holmes finally opened his eyes and engaged the priest directly. "The men had no problem with this arrangement?"

"No, sir, they did not. All seemed to enjoy her company. And if allowed this one discretion, Miss Mary is a quite handsome young lady and wonderful at conversation with a good sense of humour. And I believe her accent adds to her allure. I doubt many men, regardless of their difference in class, would find fault in letting her sit at their table."

"I see. Did anyone leave the room for any reason during the meal?"

"Miss Mary was always in and out, serving and taking plates. She would sit and eat and converse a bit then be up doing it all over again. I believe Ramsey got up and helped her once to bring in some dishes. That was it. The rest of the time we were all together. Miss Mary cleared the table while we said our goodbyes, and off they went to hunt."

"What time was that?"

He thought for a moment. "About close on seven this morning, I suspect. They came back from hunting empty-handed, and I set up for Mass shortly after they arrived at half-past nine as was our custom."

"What of the others?" Holmes asked. "What do you know of them?"

"They are all very close friends. Ramsey, John, Harold, Oliver, and William have grown up together. Their families are all close and I believe distantly related. Through governesses, school, and university they have been inseparable."

Holmes stopped the priest. "You have mentioned four friends of Ramsey, yet only three bodies are here. Who is the William that seems to be the one friend missing?"

With his trembling hand wiping his flushed and sweaty cheeks Father Harrison said, "That is the only anomaly on the entire morning, now that I am pushed to recall it. Ramsey said that William—William Waverly—has been away, it seems. They were all to go to London for some function given by Ramsey's father. The assumption of the others was that William went early, and he would meet up with them when they arrived on Thursday morning. He tends to be a free spirit that way and is less tethered to the group than the rest."

"How long has he been absent?" Holmes asked.

"Only a few days I believe."

"Please be honest with me when I ask this next question," my friend then said with much solemnity. "It will do you no good to lie."

"Of course," the priest replied weakly.

"Did you partake of the wine?"

Harrison seemed offended at the question. "Of course, I did. It is the Blood of Christ, why would I not partake?"

"And everyone else did, as well?" pressed Holmes.

He was silent for a moment then sighed and went on. "I believe so. At their age, Mr. Holmes, it can be hard sometimes to completely get the boy out of the man. You see, there are times when they will completely consume the contents of the chalice before it gets to Miss Mary. They do it in jest, but it is a cruel thing to do, and I admonish them when it happens."

"Did it happen today?" Holmes asked.

He nodded as he wiped his flushed cheeks once again. "But you consume the whole Christ in the Eucharist, so it would not matter if you didn't partake of the wine. I do believe, however, that there were a few drops left when she drank."

It was at this point that we were interrupted by Constable Milks. "I am sorry, Mr. Holmes, but we will have to cut this interview short." He held up a small, clear, glass vial with a small amount of a milky fluid still within. "This was found in the pocket of your coat, reverend, which was hanging on a hook in the entranceway of the rectory. Now, I am sure I don't know my poisons as well as Mr. Holmes, here, but the smell to me says he was right when he guessed hemlock." He pulled the priest up from the pew by the arm. "You are coming with us, Mr. Harrison, on suspicion of murder."

"I did not do this!" the priest implored. "As God is my witness!"

"Well, unless the Almighty comes down here in person to vouch for you, our evidence says otherwise." Milks then turned to us. "I apologize, Mr. Holmes, that this wasn't much of a puzzle to solve. I guess you shall have all your time back to visit your friend."

Milks and another constable led the priest down the center aisle.

"So that is that?" I asked.

Holmes ascended the altar. "You know me, Watson. *That* is never that."

On the left side of the altar was a small table with a gold chalice and crystal decanter of wine. "The authorities took the vial, but they were derelict in leaving the chalice and wine." He sniffed the decanter and frowned. "Hemlock, almost certainly. It has a bit of a mousey smell. But why poison the whole decanter? Why not just the chalice alone? He certainly had the opportunity with his back to the congregation. That is very suggestive."

I thought momentarily then offered, "If only the chalice was poisoned that would suggest the murderer was more particular of his victim, but if the whole decanter was poisoned that would mean that the killing was more indiscriminate."

"Precisely, Watson. I do not think the priest is the murderer."

"And it is obvious that he, too, is having ill-effects from drinking, with his sunken, grey features and profuse sweating," I added. "Why would he poison himself?"

"And why would this murderous letch," he said with sarcasm, "be so foolish as to leave the poison in his coat, sure to be found by the curious constabulary? Come, Watson. Let us examine where the poison was found."

At the west end of the church, just beyond the first set of pews, we were shown through a small hallway that opened into the rectory by one of the many constables. At the end of the hallway the room opened into a large entranceway with the front door on the right, a coat rack with the priest's overcoat still hanging adjacent to the door, and a large secretary's desk just beyond the coat rack. Other rooms opened off that small greeting area.

Holmes noticed something on the marble floor in front of the door. "Ah, Watson, a partial footprint. A left, I believe."

The constable with us, said, "The priest's, no doubt. The yard around is rather muddy from all the rain the past few days."

Holmes said nothing.

He next wanted to inspect the secretary's desk, but the constable cautioned him. "You may look only, sir. Nothing is to be touched or handled in any way."

"Yes, that does seem to be how investigations are handled here," Holmes mumbled to me, as he looked over the desk.

After a cursory glance, he turned and walked quickly back through the hallway into the church with me at his heel.

"Did you see anything of note?" I asked.

"You know me, Watson. My eyes tend toward that which is ignored. The shoe print was not Harrison's. His shoes are soft-soled with tread and a rounded toe. The print on the floor had no tread and a pointed toe."

"A dress shoe," I finished.

As we turned and went back up the center aisle, he added, "In lieu of a miraculous Providential appearance, I think Father Harrison will have to make do with us. Come, we shall look in on good, old Whympenny for a bit, then let us see what we can do about these murders."

. . . . .

Phineas met us at the door with a smile and a sweep of his giant arm bidding us enter. "Come, come, gentlemen. You must sit and tell me of the mischief happening on my doorstep. Sherlock, it is so nice to see you again!"

Holmes chuckled, "Phin, as robust as ever, I see."

"Yes, the clean, country air has not, unfortunately, deterred my love of food. If I have my way, when I go to that Great Beyond it shall be with a pastry stuffed between my cheeks!"

A bit breathless, he forced himself into a rose carved, balloon-back chair. "We have plenty of time to talk food. For now, though," he added with anticipation, "indulge this fat, old man and tell me what is what across the way."

Holmes succinctly relayed what we had learned, and afterward, Phineas said, "There has been something brewing over there for some time now. That it ended like this is not surprising to me."

"Oh, really? Why?" asked Holmes, interest peaked, brow askew.

"If you don't already know, Miss Mary, as she is wont to be called, is a very pretty young lady. If I were forty years younger and possessed a bit less girth—"

"You would cook her dinner then eat it all yourself," I finished.

He nodded his head and laughed. "Touché, John. Let us then stick to fact and not fantasy. As you can see, I have a perfect view of the church through my front window here."

"And you have seen things," Holmes anticipated.

"Some things. Not much. But enough to know that something like this was coming."

Holmes was going to interject something, but Phin cut him off with a sausage-sized finger, "*Such as* the Montfort boy showing some affection to that lovely Miss Mary right out in front of the church. It was dusk, and they thought it too dark for anyone to see. But I was blessed with the eyes of an owl. They embraced and kissed. The whole affair was over in a second, maybe two. Anyone else would not have noticed."

I asked, "How do you go from a brief moment of intimacy to murder?"

Phin smiled wide on that full-moon face of his. "Because he was not the only admirer she cozied up to, that's how."

I gasped. "Which of the other young men was she playing?"

"The barrister's son, Will Waverly."

"Who, coincidentally, was absent from the group today," Holmes replied somberly. "That is a dangerous game to play between friends, the effects with which she is now dealing. Was there one that she hoisted her affections upon more than the other?"

"I only witnessed a little slice of the pie—if I may use that turn-of-phrase because I am famished, but from the goings-on that I could see over this summer past in that little alcove, away from prying eyes, I would say that it was the Montfort boy who finally won her over. She spent more time in intimate conversation with him, touching him on the arm innocently, but not so innocently. Their close-in conversations, almost nose to nose," he added almost rapturously. "I could tell that she brightened considerably in his company. With that recessed entranceway and those two large rhododendrons on either side of the steps, no one would have been a witness to any of it but me. Nonetheless, as I have previously stated, I am sure I have seen but a small part of a larger and much darker picture."

"You have managed to see much just the same," I replied.

"As you can see, my cottage is almost directly across from the church. All other homes are too far away at angles to see what goes on in that cloistered little nook. And I believe the empty land on the other side gave them a false sense of security. Since I rarely go outside, they forget I am here, a man of my size, if you can believe that. So, I got a front-row seat to these little affairs. Without friends with which to pass the time," He went on, feigning melancholy, "that was my only little bit of theater…oh how I miss the Lyceum," he lamented.

I laughed, "It seems you kept company just fine, my dear fellow, and their names were pumpernickel and Bechamel!"

Phin laughed heartily, which was warming to see, but Holmes's features darkened. "Jesting aside," he replied with sagacity, "if you could see her delight being in Mr. Montfort's company, then it isn't a far reach to think Waverly may have seen it, as well."

"And I also believe the priest must have known something," Phin added, "probably through their confessions if they are good Catholics. I saw him one afternoon imploring her about something, hands upon both shoulders. She had just come through the front doors, but he was right on her heels. She gave him a curt response, shook herself loose, then walked away. That was about two months ago."

"Did you see anything untoward today?" Holmes asked.

Phin replied, "I only saw them as they returned from their hunt."

"Did you happen to see anyone at the rectory door at any point today?"

"I did not," was the reply.

"How does it all fit together?" I finally implored. "Did William Waverly find out he was being duped and in a jealous rage poison his friends and his would-be love? Why everyone and not just Montfort? And why was the poison found in Father Harrison's coat pocket?"

"Maybe this Waverly boy is casting dispersions elsewhere by setting up the priest," Phin offered with delight, rubbing his meaty hands together.

Holmes gazed out the window at the grey day outside and was silent for a long moment. Rising, he said finally, "You relish too much the game, my dear Phin, but forget four are dead and possibly a fifth before the day is through. Come, Watson, the tangled mess in which we find ourselves has become more raveled. It is now time to attempt its unraveling."

"And in the meantime, how does pressed duck sound for dinner?" asked our portly friend. "A special press I had ordered from Paris just arrived, and I am dying to try it out."

"Salad and a few cold meats should be sufficient for all of us," said I in my doctorly voice.

Holmes and Phin both groaned at the statement.

. . . . .

Phin gave us the use of his dogcart, and since I had already spent two weeks in Woodford-Upon-Lea, I knew my way around the place well enough. Phin knew where the Waverly place was due to their prominence as the area's largest law firm. He gave us the directions, and we proceeded there.

The village shared resources with the bigger Crofton Barrow a few miles away. The Waverly family occupied a large corner brownstone in the middle of town there. When we knocked, a dowdy, rosy-cheeked lady answered the door.

Holmes bowed slightly. "Good afternoon, madame. I am Sherlock Holmes, and this is my associate Dr. Watson. We are here on a matter of police business and are hoping to speak to Mr. William Waverly if he is in."

Her cheeks flushed impossibly more. "Oh, I do hope everything is alright, sir. But Mr. William isn't in at present. Is he in trouble?"

"Is *trouble* routinely the sort of thing Mr. Waverly would be in?"

"Oh no, sir," she said rather unconvincingly. "It's just that, well…on a few occasions, his temper has gotten the best of him, as has happened with all of us I'm sure. On the whole, he is a good lad."

"An angel, no doubt," Holmes quipped, grinning politely, "No madame. He is in no trouble, but we have some questions to ask that involve his friends and the new church in Woodford."

"St. Anne's, yes I know the church. They all go there regularly. Is everything alright?"

"As I said, madame," Holmes reiterated, trying to hide his irritation, "he is in no trouble at all, or it would not be me at your door, it would be Constable Milks, no doubt."

Relief slackened the features on the woman's face. "Well, Mr. William, I assume, is in London. He and his friends were supposed to attend an event for some function of Sir Montfort."

"You *assume*?"

"Well, the event wasn't supposed to be for two more days, this Thursday, and I know I have seen Mr. Ramsey with the other lads he goes about with. It is very unlike any of them to go anywhere without the others, thick as thieves, they are; but this Saturday past, I heard him tell his father at dinner that he was going to London with his friends for the Sir Montfort event on Thursday, but the next day he was gone. Why he left before the rest of them is beyond me, but he sometimes likes his own company best and goes about on his own."

"Did he pack an overnight bag?" Holmes asked.

"I never thought to check. We had a loss to the staff recently, and I have been picking up the extra work until we hire more help. But, like I said, Mr. William is a bit like the wind and comes and goes as he pleases, so it never occurred to me to look."

"Would it be possible for us to take a look in his room?"

"I am not permitted to let anyone in when the house is empty of its owner, which it presently is, but if you are willing to wait, I shall go up to his room and look. I shan't be but a minute."

A few minutes later she returned with a worried look upon her face. "His valise is still in his room."

Holmes asked, "Was it out as though he were about to use it and was perhaps called away before getting a chance to pack?"

"No, sir," she shook her head vigorously. "It was still put away. It's as though he left without even thinking to pack…and I think it was because of this." She handed Holmes a card which smelled faintly of roses. On it was one word: Come. "I found it on his writing desk."

"Do you know when this was delivered?" Holmes asked.

"I do not. I have never seen this card." Her face deepened its rosy hue, once more. "Oh dear. What does this all mean?"

My friend gave her a reassuring smile. "I am sure there is a logical explanation for it, and he will soon be at home once more. Please tell him to get in touch with Constable Milks should he return."

He said nothing regarding the card or missing young man as we next drove over to see how Miss Mary was faring in hospital. It was at the nearer end of Crofton Barrow on the road to Woodford-Upon-Lea. When we passed it on our way to the Waverly place, I wondered why we did not stop then, but my friend has a certain order of things that others find hard to follow. I have learned to leave him to his circuitous methodologies.

We found Mary Holowczak lying in bed with pillows propping her head up. She was grey and saturated with perspiration. Her breathing was a bit laboured, and her eyes were drearily open.

When we told the head matron that we were there in an official capacity, she acquiesced, however, we were not to stay long.

"Miss Mary, I am Sherlock Holmes, and I am helping the constabulary with the unfortunate deaths of your friends and the attempt on your life. Do you feel well enough to answer just a few questions, then we shall go?"

She shook her head yes. "I look dreadful," she struggled out in a soft accent, "but I feel much better than I did a few hours ago. I am hoping the worst is over. I think something was in wine. It smelled funny when I drank."

"Yes, we believe you were all poisoned. However, my inquiry at present involves your rather intimate relationships with William Waverly and Ramsey Montfort."

Her half-closed eyes opened in surprise. "How do you know this?"

"It is my job to know," replied Holmes.

After a moment, she nodded in acquiescence with tears in her eyes. "It is lonely not being from here and having no more family. People look at you. They…say things. I am all alone now except church. They both showed interest and did not seem to care I am foreigner. I was…how you say—hedging my bets. But Ramsey won my heart and soul. It was wrong what I did and made act of contrition for my sins."

Holmes then asked, "Did you send a note to Mr. Waverly that simply said 'Come'?"

She wrinkled her brow. "No. No note."

Holmes produced the card and handed it to her. "Is this your writing upon this card?"

A look of recognition washed over her. "Oh, yes, this my card. I am teaching everyone my language. It is much fun. I make cards at home with words, English on one side and Polish on the other. I show card in English, and they say word in Polish I teach them. I show them word in Polish, and they say it in English if they remember. This one, I write *come* but must forget to put Polish word on back—*chodz*. Did you get this from Father's desk drawer in rectory? There are many cards in there. He pulls them out when everyone wants lesson."

"It was found in Mr. Waverly's room on his writing desk," Holmes replied somberly.

"But why would he want card?" the young girl asked and began to cough.

"I don't believe he took the card Miss Holowczak, I believe it was sent to him. How did the perfume come to be on it?"

Wiping her mouth with a kerchief and breathing a bit of color back into her face she replied, "I have small room and have more on my writing desk than I should. I spilled perfume on some cards. There are many that Father has that don't smell like roses. You will see if you look in his desk."

"The large one next to the rectory entrance?"

"Yes, there. He keeps them in one of the drawers."

"Turning to the relationship, did Waverly know about you and Ramsey Montfort?"

Her face grew dark, and she replied, "Yes, Ramsey told Will just recently, but he seemed already to know. He was not happy, but he is best friend of Ramsey, and they reconciled quickly. But Will grew quiet, and I could see the hate in his eyes when Ramsey was not looking."

She began to sob, and the color drained from her face. "I believe it is my fault this tragedy happened. How could I be so cruel to a person? Now all my friends are dead!" Her face suddenly went slack, and the poor girl fainted.

Running to Mary's bedside the head matron nudged me aside and said, "It is time for you to go, gentlemen. You have pushed her too far. She needs rest if she is to recover sufficiently from her near-fatal poisoning."

Rebuffed for the time being, we left. As we walked down the hallway, I voiced a notion that had been ruminating in my mind since we were at the church. "Holmes, do you not think it odd that—and I am sure you noticed this now that we've seen her—that the girl was given a different poison? She was the only one who vomited and did not die where she sat."

Holmes patted me on the back. "Bravo, Watson! You do yourself an injustice by saying that you cannot learn my methods. You are right. Miss Mary was poisoned by arsenic. The garlic smell was quite noticeable on her breath. But she ingested only a small amount. Just enough to make her sick. Another strike against the local force, which did not catch that crumb amongst the cake. I am glad I came down to see old Phin, for had I not, I fear a terrible injustice would have followed."

. . . . .

We arrived back on Phin's street after a short drive. I stopped the dog cart in front of the fifth cottage down from the church. Holmes knocked on the door, and a thin, pale, grey-haired woman answered.

"Hello, madame, I am Sherlock Holmes, and this is my colleague Dr. Watson. We are here on police business."

"Yes, the news makes its way down the street rather quickly here," she replied. "Poor Mary. I do hope she pulls through. She was a good tenant—she leaned in close—despite being, well…you know."

"No, madame, I do not," Holmes expostulated. "Are you referring to her Slavic heritage or her Catholicism?"

Her eyes widened. "Both!"

"And yet you found it in your heart to rent a room to the girl."

Sensing Holmes' sarcasm, she only replied, "As I said, she seemed a good girl. Pleasant. Has some trouble grasping English, but she is understandable enough. She keeps a small veg garden in the back for her cooking, keeps to herself, and pays on time. What more could a landlord want."

"Indeed," Holmes retorted dryly. "As I said, we are helping Constable Milks in this matter, and I was hoping to press upon your sense of civic duty and let us inspect her room."

"Let no one say that I was an obstacle to the Crown." She pulled out a ring of keys and picked one out from the six. "If you go around to the right side of the cottage, her door is the last one down. The rooms in the back have their own entrances. You can leave the keyring on her bed when finished, and I'll retrieve it later."

As Holmes unlocked the door, I gave a cursory glance over at Miss Mary's garden, which was about thirty feet away at the back of the property against a fence. The dirt was soggy and bare, with bricks and stakes and a shovel thrown over the top of it. With the growing season all but over, all the vegetables had already been picked, the last of which having probably been used in that morning's breakfast.

Once inside, the room was just as Mary said it would be—cluttered but not dirty. She had books in English, some Polish, pictures of her homeland and what I assumed was family, and true to her word, her writing desk was awash in blank cards, foolscap, and a half-used bottle of perfume.

"It looks like she enjoyed the theater, Watson," Holmes said as he looked through the contents on her dressing table. "She has been to the Queen's Theater in Crofton Barrow a few times, but most of these playbills are from her homeland, the last being—five years ago if I am reading the dates correctly." He looked through a few of them. "And it seems our Miss Mary not only liked the theater but was part of it. I do not claim an extensive Polish vocabulary, but I am somewhat familiar with it. I am quite certain this particular scribble on at least three of these playbills are Mary Holowczak in the cast."

"I wonder why she did not try her hand at theater here?" said I.

At that, there was a knock at the door that led to the interior of the home. Suddenly, the owner poked her head through the door. Rather sheepishly she said, "I couldn't help but overhear your conversation from the other side of the door, and she has, in fact, tried out for a few parts at the Queens. She and her sister both did. I overheard them preparing their auditions—"

Holmes put up his hand to stop her. "Her sister? No one mentioned a sister."

"Her sister, Anna, poor thing, has been dead for two years, now. They both shared this room. She was accosted walking home one night from Crofton Barrow. No one knows who did it. She was found dead by her sister and the priest, who both went to look for her when she didn't come home that night. Mary was in a bad way for some time, but eventually got over it, deciding that life had to go on for the living."

Angry, Holmes lamented, "Why oh why, Watson, would we not be made aware of this vital information by the constabulary! Instead, we find out from the landlady!"

He handed the woman her key ring. "Thank you, madame. You've been most helpful." Turning on his heels, he rushed for the door and exclaimed, "Come, Watson, we need to make haste before it's too late!"

"Where are we off to?" I asked as we mounted the dog cart.

"We have one stop, then we need to get back to the hospital as quickly as we can make this old horse gallop."

. . . .

When we returned to see Miss Mary, she seemed to have fully recovered from not only her faint but also the poisoning as well. Her colour was back, and she was out of bed and back in her clothes, looking alert. She was speaking to Constable Milks when we arrived.

"Ah, gentlemen, come to pay your respects? It looks like Miss Mary, here, will not only make a full recovery but leave hospital in record time. We are still trying to tie up loose ends, but I think we have this in the bag. The priest admitted that there was another friend who had been absent this morning, William Waverly, and I was just talking to Miss Mary as to any suggestions where we might look for him. It seems odd that on the day all his friends are murdered that he be absent. I believe the priest is the culprit, and Waverly might be a co-conspirator, though I admit a motive still eludes me."

"I believe I may know where William Waverly is," offered Holmes.

"Well spit it out, man. We need to speak to him."

"Since he is dead and buried in Miss Mary's garden, I doubt you will get much from him."

Mary gasped, and Milks looked wide-eyed at Holmes. "What the deuce are you talking about, sir?"

"I shall put forth what I know, and Miss Mary will have to fill in some gaps if she is willing to oblige. I shall go first."

Mary said nothing, only glowered at Holmes.

Holmes began his dissertation of the crime. "Over the course of the last two years you have been scheming to murder these five men, and what a patient schemer you are, my dear

Miss Mary. One who could rival that of any in London, save a few unique specimens."

"But why?" asked Milks.

"The *why* we shall get to, momentarily, with Mary's help. Let us stick with the *how* for a moment. She poisoned the decanter with hemlock."

"That much is known already, but the *who* in your deductions are a bit flawed Mr. Holmes," said Milks. "Don't forget why we are having this conversation in a hospital. Mary was poisoned, as well. Why would she poison herself? That is preposterous."

"And you completely missed the fact that Mary was affected by a completely different poison. She had to poison herself with arsenic instead of the hemlock in the wine, and one small grain of arsenic, easily concealed was all she needed. Much can be gleaned by asking the right questions, constable. Father Harrison relayed that the men would often, as a puerile prank, drink all the wine in the chalice before she had a chance to partake. She knew if by chance they played that little game today there would be no more poisoned wine left to drink, so she would need a backup poison to throw authorities off her trail. For, as you say, why would anyone poison themselves knowing the outcome would be their own demise?

"Indeed, Mr. Holmes. Doing that would be tantamount to suicide. You have yet to show how it can be done and why."

"Mithridatism is the how" my friend replied.

Milks *hmphed* at the statement but not before throwing an unflattering glance at the young woman, who had sat back down on the bed wearing a look of distress and anger. "What in the world is that?" he asked.

"Mithridates was an ancient king who constantly worried about being poisoned," Holmes went on. "He conquered this burden by slowly ingesting small amounts of different poisons until his body built up an immunity to them. He did this with many poisons and so was impervious to their effects. Yet, when the Romans over-ran his kingdom, and he feared being paraded through the streets in humiliation, he tried to poison himself, but the attempt was fruitless. The legend has it that a friend finally ran him through with a sword."

"And you are saying that she did this—made herself invulnerable to the poison hemlock?"

"Not just her," Holmes responded with a wagging finger. "Father Harrison, as well."

"They are in this together?" Milks asked in disbelief.

"No," Holmes replied, "But she did not want the death of the priest on her conscience. He was innocent of the crime for which she was dispensing her justice. So, she made him resistant, as well."

Milks interrupted, "Then he would be an accessory to the murders if he knew what she was planning and went along with it."

"That would indeed be true, constable, if only he knew what Miss Mary was doing. I believe that she was secretly doing it through the czarnina soup she was serving at breakfast. It was the only thing they alone ate."

"What on earth is that?" he asked.

"It is duck's blood soup. As part of the legend, it is said the way in which Mithridates accomplished becoming immune was to feed each particular poison to ducks in increasing amounts, and whichever ducks did not die he would kill and drink their blood. Miss Mary's method was a bit more tasteful than was the king's."

He looked upon the young woman with a grin. "Have I been correct thus far, Miss Mary?"

She said nothing, only stared blankly at the floor.

The constable shook his head, still in unbelief, but I could tell the reasons for not believing Holmes were quickly fading. "But she almost died. You saw how sick she was. I was told she fainted while in your company earlier. Poisoning yourself is an awful heady risk to take, knowing it might not work out the way you think it should."

Holmes smiled in that confidently smug way he does when he is in possession of all the facts. "Poison is in the dose, constable. One grain of arsenic is enough to make one visibly sick and she was. She was genuinely ill the way a bad piece of beef makes one ill. But one grain of arsenic will not kill you. Some of what you saw was authentic, the rest was acting, of which Watson and I found she and her sister were quite fond. All this evidence was at your fingertips had you not stopped your investigation once the poison was found in Harrison's coat pocket."

"So, you are saying she planted the poison on the priest? Why?"

Holmes sighed for when, even in the face of critical elucidations, the facts were not presenting themselves as clearly to the authorities as they were to him. With exasperation, he said, "This was her grand plan—please stop me, Miss Mary, if I stray from fact: She would elicit the affections of both Montfort and Waverly and play off them. She needed two men to make her plan work. She would eventually pick Montfort over Waverly as her beau, and Waverly would then become the scapegoat for everything else that happened. He seemed a bit of a bohemian, and came and went as he wished, so he would be the least likely of the friends to evoke concern for his absence. With Waverly gone from the group during the poisoning and whose affections were eventually spurned by Mary for Montfort's, you now have a second viable suspect. With an alternative explanation of the facts, and with no obvious motive, she knew you would eventually have no choice but to let the priest go. It would have just been a waiting game. And to that end, she even gave you Waverly's footprint in the entranceway. Even a cursory examination of the priest's footwear would have shown the print wasn't his. More proof that the man you would never find was setting up the priest for the fall. I do not think she had much time to hide it, so with a careful search of the grounds, I would wager the finding of that shoe."

"All very elaborate," Milks finally agreed, "but what was the end game here? That piece of information is still eluding me."

"It is because Mary thinks that her sister died at the hands of these five young men."

The young woman finally looked up, face reddened in anger. "They did kill her. I hear them. I hear their confessions to Father Harrison. I hear Will tell Father they pushed her out of wagon and left her to die. I wanted *zemsta*—revenge. I am patient woman. Two years it took, but I got revenge for my dear Anna."

It was at this time that Father Harrison entered the room in the company of a constable.

Milks was on the verge of objecting that a suspect in four murders was out of his cell, but Holmes put up a hand to stop his protestations.

The priest said, "Dear girl, whatever you heard, you only heard part of the confession. What happened was an accident."

Milks interjected somewhat perturbed, "We investigated that for weeks, and the whole time you knew what happened?"

"I cannot break the seal of the confessional. I will not divulge anything any of them told me of each person's particular culpability, but I think I can say, without asking for guidance from the bishop, this much—Anna was walking home from Crofton Barrow. The boys, on their way back to the village themselves after a social gathering, offered her a ride, and she agreed. At some point, she became… uncomfortable sitting next to one of them and asked to change seats with the boy across from her. She stood to change seats. At that point, the carriage wheel hit a divot in the road. She lost her balance and fell from the wagon, landing awkwardly on her head. They stopped to render aid, but it was too late. She had broken her neck and died instantly in the fall. At the vehement request of one, they decided that it would be better for them to keep quiet. They'd all had a bit too much to drink, and one in particular was worried that because of some past indiscretions that involved the authorities, they might not believe the story. There was nothing they could do to save her, and there was no need for anyone to know of their involvement, even though, as I said, it was an accident."

"And how do we know they were telling you the truth?" Milks asked.

Harrison said, "In confession, there is no reason to lie. Your confession is to God, not to me. God already knows the truth."

"You are telling this now? Why did you not tell me this then?" Mary asked with anger lacing her words.

"They did not come to me until a month after it happened. By that point you had shown the beginnings of moving on with your life, and knowing the truth, even though it had been an accident, I felt your recovery from the loss of your sister would have digressed. Plainly put, I did not want to reopen such a fresh wound. I had no idea you overheard any of the confessions."

"And now you find out that your revenge was for what, an accident?" Milks interjected.

Wiping away her tears, Mary replied, "Their silence alone was deserving of the noose."

"Well this didn't end the way I thought it would," said Milks as he put Mary in cuffs. With a note of acquiescence, he then asked, "And where again did you say Waverly was?"

"Buried in the garden behind the cottage where she rents a room. His will be the corpse with the missing shoe."

I would have laughed at Holmes' remark had the situation not been so grim.

Holmes pulled out the card and handed it to Milks. "I believe she enticed Waverly to her room with this note. It is one of many cards you will find in Harrison's desk in the rectory. She made the cards to teach them all her native language. When Waverly saw the one word, he knew its author and where to go. When he arrived, it was probably nightfall. When she saw him coming down the walkway to her door, she called him back to the garden where she struck him with a brick or a shovel and quickly buried the body in a grave she no doubt had already dug for him in the fresh, loose soil while she awaited his arrival."

As Milks led Mary away, she stopped momentarily in front of Father Harrison. She looked so sorrowful. "If you knew I hear some of confession, would you have broken the seal and tell me truth about my Anna, then?"

The priest thought for a moment then said, "No."

Milks led her away and said over his shoulder, "You're free to go Reverend."

When we were alone, Holmes engaged Father Harrison. "You lied to her. You would have relayed everything had she asked."

"You are right, Mr. Holmes, but why let her know that her fate could have been changed. She would spend her remaining days wondering *what if* instead of *what now*. For her, the *what now* is more important and what she needs to focus on." He sighed a deep, sorrowful sigh. "If I had known this was to be the ending, I would have forsaken my vows altogether to save those six souls. I can't help but feel I have let them all down."

"Yet, on at least one occasion you were seen in a heated discussion with the girl in the front alcove. My guess is you saw how she was playing both men and warned her of the possible consequences?"

"You are correct, once again, Mr. Holmes. It was not fair to her or either man doing what she was doing. One or all would have ended up hurt in the end. Now, I must live my life having seen just how hurt all would end up being. I shall end my days on my knees in prayer over this ordeal."

"Then you are a better shepherd than you give yourself credit for," replied my friend earnestly.

. . . .

Holmes was unusually quiet as we rode back to Phin's cottage. I felt—and I knew Holmes felt—that sometimes justice seemed incomplete. An innocent man was almost incarcerated for a crime he did not commit, and a young woman, grieving the death of her sister, would hang for five deaths that did not have to happen. Too many crimes went unpunished or the wrong people punished due to powerful influences, mere folly, or both. He had many times mentioned writing a volume on his methods of deduction once he retired to his beekeeping in Sussex. It was at times like this that I wondered why he waited. The world would be without the great detective someday, yet it was now—and would always be—in dire need of his services.

To break him from this silence I spoke up for there were questions I needed answered. "Indulge me, Holmes. When did you begin to suspect Mary in all of this?"

"Poison is a woman's preferred method of murder, Watson, so I tended towards Mary from the beginning. And when I learned of Waverly's temperament, I knew he could not be the murderer. He would have bludgeoned a man before resorting to poison. Once I was provided a motive all the pieces of the puzzle fit perfectly into their rightful places."

"And how on earth did you know Waverly was buried in Mary's garden?"

Two things, Watson," said he with a satisfied air. "It was a convenient place in which the earth was already disturbed that wouldn't throw suspicion, and the middle of the garden was a full five inches higher than at the perimeter. In my experiments while at university before we were introduced, I discovered five inches is precisely the amount of displacement for a body of average build."

After a brief silence, he added, "Thank you, Watson."

"For what?"

"I prefer facts over feelings and was at a precipice. Those perfectly timed questions have brought me back."

When we finally walked through the door into Phin's cottage, wonderful aromas filled the air. Phin emerged from the kitchen, apron affixed, sweat beading on his forehead, a bit out of breath. "I am sorry, John, but salad and cold meats just will not do for us old friends. I took the liberty to use my new press on a duck, and these exquisite fragrances are the result. My mouth is watering at the thought. Please sit at the table. I have a first course that we can enjoy, and you can tell me how your investigation went. It will be like old times."

We sat at the table, and Phin brought us each a bowl of hearty, hot soup—thank goodness not duck's blood soup. The three of us ate a wonderful meal and talked about the good old days in London. It would be the last time we saw our dear friend.

The End

Other Sherlock Holmes Titles By William Todd:

The mystery of the Broken Window

A Reflection of Evil

Murder in Keswick

Victorian Horror Compilations By William Todd:

Dead of Night

Beyond the Gossamer Veil

Printed in Great Britain
by Amazon